THE TANGLED WEB

By Giles A. Lutz

THE TANGLED WEB

GILES A. LUTZ

DOUBLEDAY & COMPANY, INC.
GARDEN CITY, NEW YORK
1983

All of the characters in this book are fictitious, and any resemblance
to actual persons, living or dead, with the exception of historical
personages, is purely coincidental.

Library of Congress Cataloging in Publication Data

Lutz, Giles A.
The tangled web.

(A Double D western)
I. Title.
PS3562.U83T3   1983   813′.54
ISBN 0-385-18433-6
Library of Congress Catalog Card Number 82-45614

THE TANGLED WEB

CHAPTER 1

Hays, Kansas, was a pleasant, sleepy little town. It sat in flat, treeless country and agriculture was its chief pursuit. Without trees, it was difficult to get material for fence posts. But that hadn't stopped the farmers from fencing in their property. This was limestone country, and it lay in great layered thickness just underneath the surface. Where it outcropped it was relatively easy to get at the stone. Thick segments of the material could be chiseled off in long stretches. Then that length could be split off in six-to-eight-inch thicknesses, then cut off to seven- or eight-foot lengths that could be easily handled. Somebody had gotten the idea that the limestone could be used to replace ordinary wooden posts. The only trouble was that the stone posts were brutally heavy, weighing from a hundred and fifty pounds to four hundred pounds depending upon the thickness of the length that was being worked. It took two strong men to lift a post off a wagon and drop it into a hole dug for it.

Rowry Saxton groaned at the memory of the days he had worked with those limestone posts. My God, that was man-killing work. He had worked four summers until he was nineteen, and the hauling and tugging of that kind of weight had slowly strengthened his arms and chest. He could hold his own with anyone when it came to handling a limestone fence post. But he wasn't sorry to leave that work when the job of deputy marshal was offered to him. He had held the deputy badge for the past six years, and he saw nothing different in the future. His thoughts went back to those grueling summers. The family had needed the income the work had brought in. He remembered standing before a mirror and flexing his muscles. He wouldn't have wanted that kind of work forever, but it had done him a lot of good.

He remembered fighting a stone post off a wagon, upending it to let one end drop into a hole. Then the dirt was shoveled back into the hole and tamped against the post until nothing could budge it. Lord, how many short lengths of wire had he used to tie the barbed wire to the posts. If he had been paid only a few cents for each tie, he would be a wealthy man. It took quite a while to put up a fence, but after it was done, a man didn't have to worry about the erosion of the fence post due to the weather. That post was in the ground forever, or at least as long as the landowner wanted a fence. It took years of hard labor to construct those fences, but with the passing years, they had crawled steadily along the ground until now they stretched in all directions as far as the eye could see. This sort of fence building was one of the few chores that a farmer could luxuriate in, knowing that it wouldn't have to be done again.

This used to be corn country, but after several serious droughts and the great grasshopper plague, the farmers turned to growing wheat, a far more reliable crop than corn, for it matured before the summer months when the droughts usually came. This new planting also eliminated the threat of grasshoppers, for the insects didn't develop soon enough to be a serious threat to the young wheat.

Rowry moved effortlessly along the street. He was as thin as a rawhide thong and just about as tough. He was damned glad he had left behind the effort of growing crops, though he was grateful for the experience. It gave him an understanding of what made this community go. He shifted the rifle from his right hand to his left hand. He rarely carried a six-gun; it might be a little faster but it wasn't as accurate as a rifle. Rowry had gotten used to carrying the Winchester, and he'd be lost without it. But he rarely needed any kind of gun, for Hays was a peaceful town. Now and then some ebullient spirit got too liquored up, and Rowry had to arrest him to quell his enthusiasm. But those infrequent incidents were a welcome break in the monotony. Hardly anything exciting happened around here, and Rowry preferred it that way. He liked the small demands the slow passage through the sleepy days put on a man. Other parts of Kansas might be throbbing with excitement—the cow towns, Dodge City and Abilene, were making marks that would go down in Kansas history. But Rowry never missed the excitement. He felt lucky that he hadn't been born in one of the cow towns. According to the accounts that drifted out of some of those places, a man couldn't go to sleep and be certain he would wake up in the morning. Every now and then the local paper would publish one of the more lurid accounts; it seemed as if Abilene and Dodge City were almost proud of the legend that they served up a man with every breakfast. Some of the killings were legal and necessary, but others just sprang up from tempers growing so inflamed that the only cure was gunfire.

Rowry shook his head. He had heard men passing through Hays ask in amazement, "Does anything ever happen here? Doesn't the dullness drive you out of your mind?"

Rowry had never tried to answer those questions, though he could have said, with his whole being, "I hope it stays just the way it is." Just the task of living was hard enough, without adding the worry of an early and violent death. He liked this town and he liked his girl. He didn't want to live in fear of what was going to happen to him or her.

He whistled an old, familiar tune as he walked along the street. His job might not be the most important in the world, but it suited him. Being a deputy marshal would never set his pulses to pumping, and he didn't care. He had already accepted the fact that he would never be a wealthy man, or even a big man. He guessed he lacked ambition, and if his way of life was a simple one, it had enough problems to keep him humping. His father was a semi-invalid, and he needed all the care and attention Rowry could give him. Then there was the problem of Ord, his younger brother. Ord had never gotten into any serious trouble, but he seemed constantly on the brink of it. A frown unconsciously set Rowry's face. Ord was five years younger, and he was a belligerent kid, always pushing the limits of authority. Just keeping Ord in line was enough of a chore to keep Rowry occupied, and he didn't even like Ord very much. It had been that way almost from the day Ord was born. Was his dislike a form of jealousy? Rowry had asked himself that question dozens of times. Ord had been a favorite of both of their parents. The old man had taken over that feeling even after Rowry's mother had died. Rowry had tried to like him. He had tried to protect him all through school, but the more he did for Ord, the more Ord seemed to resent him. Ord was too cocksure, and he was constantly testing Rowry to see how far he could go. He had grown worse in the last couple of years. Someday there was going to be a tremendous clash between them, and right now Rowry couldn't see how it was going to come out. He seemed to be caught in a vise: he had to protect his mother's memory and his father's well-being, but Ord in his blind, stubborn way insisted upon plowing ahead. One of these days he would come up against something he couldn't bull through. Rowry didn't know what that would be, but he felt sure it was going to be a disaster for the Saxton family. Ord refused to work, had avoided it for as long as Rowry could remember. He couldn't see how Ord got along as well as he did. He suspected that Pa was giving him money that Rowry earned.

Rowry scowled. He didn't like Ord's choice of friends or what he did with them. Ord ran around with three particularly close friends, and he and Rowry had had heated words about them. If those four weren't actually engaged in something illegal, Rowry felt certain they would be before long. One of these days he might have to arrest Ord and the others. Maybe subconsciously he wished it would happen. It would be one sure way to remove Ord from the scene; then perhaps things would settle down to the calm and quiet he longed for. He shook his head and sighed. He didn't want it to come to that, but as sure as it would rain before the year ended, Rowry felt it was bound to happen.

He was passing Brown's Saloon when Elmer Brown ran out and stopped him. Brown was a short, pudgy man, now with a distraught look on his face. "My God, Rowry," he gasped. "Am I glad to see you."

Rowry stopped, his craggy features going stern. "What's happening, Elmer?"

"Chubby Inman is drunk again. You know how he is when he has too much to drink."

Rowry nodded. He had arrested Inman a dozen times for the same offense. Fines and confinement didn't seem to straighten Inman out. When he sobered up, he was filled with contrition, promising he would leave drink alone. For a few weeks, sometimes even longer, he seemed to be able to keep his promise, then something set him off again.

Rowry turned his head as a series of shots rang out. Brown quivered at each shot. "That's him," he said. "He's been getting meaner and uglier. He told me that he was going to blast the hell out of my place. Oh God," he wailed, as a couple of shots took out the big front window. "He's going to break me. I ran out just as he pulled his gun. I never was so glad to see you coming along."

Rowry shifted his rifle, hitched up his belt, and said, "Guess I'd better go in and cool him off."

"He won't listen," Brown warned.

"Then I'll have to find a way to convince him," Rowry said calmly.

He shouldered the swinging doors aside, with Brown at his heels. This wasn't the busy time. Brown had only a half-dozen customers, and they were huddled in a corner. Nobody knew how far Inman would go when he drank himself into this kind of shape.

Inman stood before the bar, a huge man with a red, bloated face and a belly that hung over his belt. He was reloading his gun, taking cartridges out of his pocket.

Rowry regarded him closely. It was amazing what liquor could do to a man. Ordinarily, Inman was a mild-mannered merchant with a fairly successful business. When he was under the influence, he was a wild man. This was the first time Rowry had ever seen him with a gun.

He walked up to him. "This is kinda expensive fun, ain't it, Chubby?"

Inman flashed him a look out of his red-rimmed eyes. Those eyes reminded Rowry of a wild animal caged up for the first time. He felt pity for this huge, soft man. Inman fought liquor like he would an enemy. It's worse than an enemy, Rowry thought soberly. It's doing its best to destroy him.

Inman thumbed in another shell, then snapped the cylinder shut. "What do you mean, expensive?" he growled. "I'm not paying for it."

"You will," Rowry said firmly. "Do you know how much that front window costs? More than you take in in a week."

"Then add the backbar mirror to my bill," Inman snarled. He whirled and faced the back mirror, bringing up his gun as he did. He emptied the pistol into the mirror. The shots shattered the mirror, and pieces of it crashed against the floor.

Brown moaned deep in his throat. He was standing clear across the room, but Rowry heard him even at that distance. Rowry could guess what ran through Brown's head. He was thinking how much the mirror and the front window cost.

Inman swung about to face Rowry. "What do you say about that, Deputy?" he snarled.

Rowry sighed. A drunk was always a dangerous person to handle because he was so unpredictable. A drunk was beyond the reach of reason, and it was difficult to hurt him because he was almost immune to pain. If a drunk was ever to be handled, it had to be done quickly and thoroughly.

"You are a hardheaded bastard, Chubby," Rowry said softly. He raised the rifle and rapped its barrel across Inman's head. He spared no force. He wanted this over with as soon as possible.

The barrel made a dull sound as it landed against Inman's head just at the hairline. Inman's eyes went wild and bulging, and his hands rose instinctively. For a long moment, he remained erect, then his legs buckled under him and he crumpled to the floor. He landed face down and with a final, convulsive effort managed to turn over. He lay on his back, his eyes unseeing. A trickle of blood ran down from the hairline, staining his face.

Rowry bent over and retrieved the pistol Inman had used. He felt better after he tucked the pistol under his belt. He stood there gazing reflectively at the huge, limp bulk. Handling that much inanimate weight was going to be a chore.

Inman's fall was like a signal, releasing all the tongues in the room. A babble of talk broke out, followed by nervous laughter. It was a relief to a man to know that Inman was harmless. A man never knew what could happen when a drunk had a gun in his hand.

Brown came up to Rowry, and his forehead was moist, but his eyes were returning to normal. "Damn, but I'm glad you were around to handle him," he said vindictively. "He did enough damage before you stopped him."

"More than enough," Rowry agreed. "Wonder what set him off this time."

Brown shook his head. "I don't know unless it was a row he had with his wife. When he started, he said something about his wife picking on him. I wish to God he'd picked another saloon."

"If you're thinking about the damage, he's good for it. He always has been."

"I know that," Brown said morosely. "I'm thinking of the time I'll lose while the window and mirror are being replaced. I'll probably have to shut down during that time."

"Charge him for that, too," Rowry said and grinned.

Brown's face brightened. "That's an idea. By God, I'm going to do it. It makes no sense for me to have to suffer because Inman drank himself crazy. What are you going to do with him, Rowry?"

"Take him to jail," Rowry said flatly. "He'll draw some time for this little escapade. That's going to cost him, too. His store will be closed while he's locked up. Seems just one of these little tricks would be enough to convince him to stay off the whiskey. I guess his kind never learn."

Brown had one idea in his mind. "With all his weight, he's going to be rough for you to handle. You'll need every man here to help carry him to the jail."

Rowry shook his head. He had considered the problem and discarded the idea of trying to carry Chubby the block and a half to jail. "You got a short length of rope around here, Elmer?"

Brown's eyes were puzzled. "Hell, you won't have to worry about him resisting for a while. You don't need to tie him up."

Rowry's temper was wearing thin. Brown was a talkative man; he could stand here and chatter about this the rest of the day if Rowry let him. "If you've got that rope, get it," he snapped. "I intend to drag Inman to jail."

Brown whistled. "I'm telling you, you'll have to work like a horse. I'm not even sure you can do—"

"Will you get that rope?" Rowry asked wearily.

Brown nodded. "I think I've got some in the storeroom. I'll be right back." He trotted off.

Rowry leaned against the bar, looking at Inman. The trickle of blood had strengthened. Maybe he had hit Inman too hard. He didn't want that. He moved away from the bar and leaned over Inman. He was relieved as he listened to the man's breathing. It might be a little on the shallow side, but it was regular enough. He didn't have to worry about Inman not pulling through. But the bleeding would have to be stopped. That could be taken care of after he got Inman to the jail.

Brown came back with a length of rope. Rowry judged it to be fourteen or fifteen feet long. It would be more than enough for what he needed. He tested the rope in his hands and nodded. It was hell for stout.

He turned Inman over, grunting as he struggled with the weight. He made a rough harness that went over Inman's shoulders and arms, knotting it securely. It left him about seven feet of rope. That gave him plenty of room to drag Inman behind him.

"You sure you can do it?" Brown asked.

Rowry picked up the short length of rope and tugged on it. "We'll know in a moment, won't we?"

For an instant, he didn't think he'd be able to move that hulk, and the cords in his neck stood out under the strain; then slowly Inman's body began to move after him. Rowry's grin was mirthless. "I'll make it."

CHAPTER 2

Rowry put his rifle under his armpit and backed through the swinging doors, dragging Inman after him. Outside, he turned and pulled Inman after him. It reminded him of handling those heavy limestone fence posts. Once he got started, things went easier. He grinned wryly, thinking that the dragging would wear away the clothes from Inman's backsides. He couldn't help it. Inman had asked for this punishment when he kept on pouring down the drinks.

The queer spectacle drew quite a few curious people, and they fell in behind Rowry and Inman. Some of them made obscene remarks, but Rowry closed his ears to them. It couldn't last too long; the jail wasn't that far away.

He was glad he didn't have to drag Inman any great distance. That would wear out a stout mule. He was glad, too, that there were no steps leading up to the building housing the jail. Getting that limp weight up steps could be beyond him. He stopped momentarily as he reached the door, turned, and faced the rowdy crowd.

"Show's over," he said. "Clear away."

A few of the brasher ones tried to make a few more clever remarks, and Rowry's steel-gray eyes pinned them down. "I meant what I said, boys. Unless you want to join Chubby in a cell."

They tried to meet Rowry's eyes and couldn't. They began drifting away until Rowry was left alone with his burden. He bent over, retrieved the rope, and dragged Inman into the office.

The noise of the bumping progress caught Creed Butler's attention, and he looked up from his desk, his eyes widening.

"What the hell?" he spluttered.

Rowry grinned. "Bringing in a customer. Only way I could get him here. He was in an argumentative mood. You didn't expect me to carry him here, did you?"

Butler shook his head and stood up. He was well into his fifties, and his hair was graying. Once, he had been a famous lawman, making a name for himself in several of the most boisterous Kansas towns. He had stopped many an argument—with his fists and with his gun. Without official explanation he had quit his job in Dodge City and appeared in Hays, Kansas, a week later. The town officials had flocked around him and offered him the badge as marshal of Hays.

Butler flatly turned them down. "I've had a belly full of trouble," he said brusquely. "I'm tired of looking down the gun barrel of some liquored-up cowboy. One day I said to myself, To hell with it, and turned in my badge. I came to Hays looking for a little peace and quiet. I don't want your job."

The outright refusal only whetted the authorities' appetites. They needed a marshal. The former one had retired because of old age. Here was their opportunity to get a famous man. They whittled on Butler for a solid month before they finally wore him down. "You can hire anybody you want as your deputy," they promised. "You wouldn't have to do anything here. Nothing ever happens in Hays."

Maybe that last argument won Butler over. Rowry was nineteen at the time, and he was one of several applicants for the deputy's badge. Out of all those applicants, Butler had hired him. Later, Butler told him why. "You were a quiet kid. You sat there and listened. The others were trying to convince me how good they were. They worked too hard at it."

"You might have picked the weakest one," Rowry suggested.

Butler had snorted and pinned on the deputy's badge. They had gotten along well, the bond between them growing daily. They could sit for long hours without a word being exchanged between them, and it only strengthened their sense of companionship. Butler had once remarked, "Rowry, one of these days, maybe in a year or two, I'll be handing in my badge. That'd put you in line for it. How'd you like that?"

Rowry had considered it. "That'd be kinda nice," he admitted. "But I'm not eating myself up until that day comes."

Butler had nodded in approval. "Maybe that's why I like you so much, Rowry. I don't have to keep looking behind me to see if you're sneaking up on me."

Butler came around the desk and looked down at Inman's face. "Not him again. He's getting to be a damned nuisance."

"Looks like it," Rowry said. "He was really packing a load this time. Brown ran out of his saloon and stopped me. He had every right to look scared. Inman had just started shooting up Brown's Saloon. I went in and confronted him."

"That was damned dangerous," Butler said disapprovingly. "A man never knows which way a drunk is likely to turn. He could just as easily put one of those bullets in you."

"Maybe," Rowry conceded. "But he was too interested in seeing how much damage he could do."

Butler cocked his head as he studied the still figure. "Just looking at him, you'd never guess there was that much violence in him. What set him off this time?"

"I don't know," Rowry said. "Brown said Inman was talking about his wife before he started getting wild. Maybe there was some kind of an argument between them. Chubby emptied his pistol into the backbar mirror. I whacked him on the head when his gun was empty. Maybe I hit him harder than I intended. I opened up his head pretty good."

Butler snorted. "You didn't hit him hard enough. Damn, how I detest a drunk. They can hurt you, and it takes a lot of hurting them before they're stopped. I'd better get Doc Swanson in here to see about that gash in Inman's head." He stepped to the door and yelled at a couple of idlers who had stopped in front of the jail and were staring curiously at it. "One of you go and get Doc Swanson," Butler bellowed at them. He came back to where Rowry stood and said, "Let's get him locked up before he comes to. He might try to take it out on both of us."

They took hold of the rope, and together they dragged Inman down the corridor. They had their pick, for the jail was empty. Butler unlocked one of the doors, then unceremoniously rolled Inman into the cell. He clanged the door shut. "Man, he's a tub of lard," he said between hard breaths. "You dragged him all the way from Brown's Saloon?"

Rowry shrugged. "It had to be done. I didn't want to fool with the customers in the saloon."

Butler looked at him with new respect. "You're stouter than I thought. Next time I hear of somebody needing a strong mule, I'll recommend you. You might be able to pick up a few extra bucks."

Rowry grinned self-consciously. "I'm not looking for anything extra. Do you think we should try to do something about Inman's bleeding?"

Butler frowned. "What could we do? Outside of washing the blood away. No, we'll wait until Swanson gets here."

They walked back to the outer office and flopped into chairs. "You did a neat job," Butler complimented Rowry. "You stopped what could have been a bad situation."

"I feel kinda sorry for him," Rowry confessed. "What's going to happen to him, Creed?"

Butler shrugged. "He'll go through the usual routine. He'll have to face a judge and plead to a drunk and disorderly charge. There's also the charge of destroying property. With his past record of drinking, it'll go harder on him this time. Damn, I wish the judge would send

him away for a good, long time. Maybe that would straighten him
out. But I doubt it. His kind never change. He'll just keep on swilling
it down until he winds up hurting somebody bad." He shook his head
at Rowry's disapproving expression. "You don't agree? I've seen
men killed because of some drunk's rage. Do you want that to happen here?"

Rowry shook his head. "You know I don't. Poor Chubby. He's
not a bad man."

"No," Butler agreed. "Just a weak one. I've seen too many of his
kind before. I learned a long time ago never to waste time mourning
for them. They picked their road. Nobody shoved them down it."

Rowry sat there in sober reflection. Everything Butler said was
probably right. "Creed, will he have to pay for the damage he did to
Brown's Saloon?"

"A cinch," Butler said flatly. "Maybe he can't afford it. That's the
judge's lookout." He started to add something, but a pudgy man hurried in and interrupted him. Doctor Swanson was overweight and had
heavy jowls. His legs looked incapable of carrying his weight. He was
breathing hard and his face was flushed. He sank down in a chair and
murmured, "I shouldn't have tried to hurry so much. Creed, could I
have a glass of water?"

Butler poured a glass of water and handed it to Swanson. "There
was no need for that kind of hurry," he said sardonically. "Inman's
just got a split head. He was bleeding when we locked him up."

Swanson snorted indignantly. "Then Benson got it all wrong when
he came after me. He said somebody was shot. All he could talk
about was all the bleeding. I thought one of you two had shot a man.
You know how I feel about guns."

Butler grinned wickedly. "We oughta know. You've raved enough
about gunshot wounds. Chubby was drunk and raising hell. Rowry
rapped him over the head with his rifle barrel. You don't approve of
that, either? How would you have handled a drunk? Slapped him on
the wrist?"

"Just the way Rowry handled it," Swanson retorted. "He could
have been hurt going up against a drunk."

"Or dead," Butler snapped. "I'm glad to hear you think we do
something right."

Rowry didn't want them getting into a heated argument. "Doc," he interrupted. "Is there any way to stop Chubby's drinking?"

"Not that I know," Swanson replied. "I've seen a lot of them. Once they get a craving for drink, nothing seems to stop them from getting their hands on a bottle." He finished his glass of water and got to his feet. "Maybe I'd better go take a look at him."

"I think that would be smart," Butler said. He and Rowry followed Swanson to the cell. Inman had regained consciousness. He sat in a huddled mass, his head cradled in his hands, and it looked as though the strength to get to his feet wasn't in him. He didn't look up until Swanson said, "At it again, Chubby? You never learn, do you?"

Inman moaned and rocked his head back and forth. He looked mournful and contrite. "I didn't intend to drink that much when I started, Doc. Just enough to get the taste of an argument between Maude and me out of my mouth. She's been nagging at me for the past two days. I just couldn't stand it anymore."

"Always blaming somebody else, aren't you, Chubby?" Swanson said. He opened his bag and removed a few items. "Let me look at that head."

He made his examination, then glanced at Rowry. "Hit him a good lick, didn't you?"

Rowry bristled at the implied criticism. "What the hell did you want me to do, kiss him?"

"I didn't mean it that way," Swanson said. He dabbed with a wad of cotton and said with satisfaction, "The bleeding's almost stopped. I'll need some water to clean him up."

"I'll get it," Rowry offered.

He hurried to the office and, after a little searching, came up with a pail. He filled it half full, then retraced his steps. "Best I could do, Doc," he said apologetically.

Swanson glanced frowningly at the pail. "It'll do," he said.

"What the hell did you expect, Doc?" Butler asked. "That we should keep the proper clean basins for hospital attention?"

"I said it'd do," Swanson snapped.

Rowry sighed. Swanson didn't like Butler, and he made no attempt to disguise it. Butler had talked to Rowry about it quite a while back. "Doc doesn't like a gunman," he had said.

"You're no gunman," Rowry protested. "You're a lawman."

"But I use a gun. It's all the same to Swanson. He's a hardheaded old cuss."

That conversation had stuck in Rowry's mind. Perhaps Swanson put him in the same class as Butler.

Swanson soaked a wadded-up piece of cloth in the water, then gently washed the cut. He had to cut away some of Inman's hair to be able to cleanse the wound thoroughly. Rowry looked glumly at the exposed gash. It was a good six inches long. He hadn't realized that he had struck with such force.

"It's a good thing you've got a hard head, Chubby," Swanson said.

"Are you saying that Rowry used too much force?" The heat was back in Butler's voice.

"I didn't say anything of the kind," Swanson flared. "I merely made a remark. But it isn't very pretty, is it? He could have broken Chubby's skull."

"Stop it, you two," Rowry said wearily.

Butler was thoroughly wound up, and he couldn't stop. "Will you tell me how he could have handled it differently?" he barked. "Chubby was shooting hell out of Brown's Saloon. Did you expect Rowry to go up to him and just beg him to stop?"

Swanson went crimson. "I didn't mean that, and you know it. Rowry, did I say any such thing?"

"No," Rowry answered. "I just wish the damned thing hadn't happened."

That wiped away Swanson's pique, and he chuckled. "I imagine Chubby feels the same way."

His deft fingers finished cleansing the wound, and he applied some kind of medicine to it. He tore off strips of plaster and affixed them over the gash. "I expect you'll have a headache for a day or two," he said.

"I've got one now," Inman said miserably. "I wish to God I'd never let Maude drive me to this."

"Don't go blaming her," Swanson said waspishly. "It was none of her doing. It was all your fault. This little episode is going to cost you. Do you know how much damage you did to that saloon?"

Inman wouldn't look at him. "I'm afraid it was a lot," he muttered.

For the first time that afternoon, Butler and Swanson were on the same side, and Butler took over. "You're damned right it was a lot," he growled. "You're going to pay for that broken front window plus the back mirror."

Inman buried his face in his hands and groaned. His hands muffled his voice, and it came out as a whisper. "It'll be a lot."

"Your store will be open for a long time without you getting anything from it," Butler said coldly. "On top of that is the fine the judge will hit you with. He may even give you some time."

"Marshal," Inman begged. "Help me out of this, and I promise you I'll never touch another drop."

"Oh, Jesus," Butler said in disgust. "How many times have I heard that?"

He stalked out of the cell and Swanson followed him. Rowry was the last, and he closed and locked the cell door.

"Rowry, I'm sorry," Inman whispered.

Rowry nodded. He could well imagine that Inman was sorry. But that sorrow couldn't do anything about the present mess. He joined Butler and Swanson in the outer office. "Send your bill, Doc," Butler said. "I'll see that the town pays you."

Swanson nodded. "No hurry."

"There won't be," Butler jeered. "Not with the town handling it."

Rowry stopped Swanson before he left. His mind still wrestled with the last words Inman had told him. "Doc, is there any hope that Chubby will change?"

"Very little, I'm afraid," Swanson answered. "A few manage to break the habit, but it takes far more strength of character than Inman has. Good day, gentlemen." He nodded and left the office.

Butler studied Rowry's face. "Something troubling you?"

"Yes," Rowry admitted. "It's just that I hate to see the mess Inman's gotten himself in. If the judge gives him time, Chubby could lose everything, including his business."

Butler shrugged irritably. "Don't sweat over it. It's not your doing. I know that's just wasted advice. You're going to chew on this day for quite a while. Why don't you take the rest of the day off? Maybe it'll clear your head."

"I'd be grateful, Creed. I want to stop by and see Abby."

Butler grinned. "I thought you would. There's nothing like a woman's consolation to salve a man's troubles."

Rowry nodded and walked out of the office. Butler was a crusty character, but he had seen a lot of life, enough to know how a man reacted to a situation.

Rowry walked down to the end of Main Street, then turned into the white-picket-fenced yard. A small white clapboard house stood in the middle of it. Abby was on her knees, digging in a flower garden. Her face was beaded with drops of perspiration and her dress was stained at the armpits.

"Rowry," she exclaimed, "I didn't expect to see you now."

She jumped to her feet and tried to do several things at once. She tried to straighten her hair, brush off her dress, and dry-wash her hands. "I look awful," she complained.

He shook his head. "You look good to me. Come here," he said and reached for her.

She tried to avoid his hands. "Not now, Rowry," she said. "Not with me looking like this."

He ignored her protests, swept her hands aside, and captured her. "I'm lucky to see you at any time." One of these days he would ask her to marry him. It was one of the inevitable things in the slow, orderly process of a man's life.

She gave in to his insistence, and he kissed her. He tasted the salt of her perspiration. She finally broke free and asked, "Did something bad happen today, Rowry?"

"What makes you ask that?" he said evasively.

"It's written all over your face. Come up on the porch and sit down out of the sun."

He followed her up the two steps and sat down in the swing. She hadn't followed suit, and he said, "Aren't you going to sit with me?"

"Not until I get some cold lemonade," she replied. She was gone before he could stop her.

It seemed she was gone forever. When she finally reappeared, she had changed her dress and brushed her hair. He took the tray laden with a pitcher of lemonade and two glasses from her hands and set it on the swing. "You didn't have to do all that," he said. She had taken time to wash her face and put on the perfume she always used. Its enticing aroma drifted to him.

"Don't tell me there's been no improvement," she said and laughed.

"I told you I liked you any way you looked. You didn't have to get all fixed up."

"I had to, Rowry. I couldn't stand myself the way I was."

He kissed her again. All this was proof to him that she cared. She had high standards for herself, and it was something he should keep in mind.

"Now, what's bothering you?" she asked, the sparkle coming back to her eyes. She was something to see, and he knew what a lucky man he was.

He moved the tray so that she could sit close to him. She filled both glasses, and Rowry sipped at his before he spoke. "I had to arrest Chubby Inman," he said slowly.

"How awful," she exclaimed. "What for?"

"For drunken and disorderly conduct," he replied gravely. "He was shooting Brown's Saloon to pieces. I had to stop him by hitting him over the head with my rifle barrel."

A frown stamped her lovely features. "I've seen him under the influence before." She was pensive for a moment before she asked, "Did you have to hurt him?"

"I split his head wide open," Rowry replied. "Then I had to drag him to jail."

She shook her head. "How awful for both of you. Is he going to be all right?"

"Doc Swanson patched him up. But I don't know how he's going to come out of this. He's got a trial to face, and he's liable for heavy damages."

"Poor Chubby," she said sorrowfully. "I've been in his store dozens of times. He's always been so pleasant."

"Unless he's been drinking," Rowry said grimly.

"Will he ever stop?"

"Swanson says he won't. Creed agrees with him."

"And it's bothering you, isn't it?" she guessed.

"I'm afraid it is. I started all this."

"You didn't. You were only doing your job. Tell me how you could have handled it differently."

He gave that some thought before he said, "I don't see how I could have."

She patted his hand. "Then quit blaming yourself, Rowry. You can't censure yourself for what another man does."

He grinned, and his entire face lighted up. "I know that. I guess I just wanted to hear that from you."

She put her head on his shoulder. "Well, you know it now."

CHAPTER 3

Rowry stayed for the better part of an hour. Lord, he felt better.

He stopped and bought a few groceries before he continued on home. Ord would never think to do anything in or out of the house. Rowry had given up trying to get anything out of him. He had used everything he could think of: reasoning, threats and promises of punishment. All of them were futile. Both he and Ord knew he wouldn't resort to abuse, particularly when their father was around. Sid Saxton had always favored Ord. If he was so blind to Ord's faults, Rowry could do nothing about it.

He walked into the house and started putting the groceries away. Sid walked haltingly into the kitchen. He was a frail man with a persistent, hacking cough. Each day Rowry thought Sid looked a little worse. The doctors said there was nothing that could be done for him. Rowry had tried to follow their explanations, but they used such odd-sounding medical terms that he was lost before they were through. All he had gotten out of it was that Sid was wasting away from a lung disease. Rowry's mother had died five years after Ord was born. She had done a lot of harm to Ord in that time, leaving a stamp of weakness on him. Ord had been a hard child to raise, filled with resentment and petulance. He fought every attempt to discipline him, and his mother had refused to let him be punished. Sid had grieved too much after she died, and he had treated Ord with the same indulgence. It was all he could do in memory of his wife.

"Have a good day?" Sid asked listlessly.

"Same as usual," Rowry replied. "You know nothing ever happens around this town."

"Do I," Sid said and sighed. "The dullness of this life would kill the strongest of men."

Rowry disagreed, but he didn't say so. If Ord wasn't in his life, he would be perfectly content. "Ord come in yet?" he asked. He didn't ask where Ord was. He doubted that Sid knew. It was useless asking questions about what Ord was doing. If Sid knew, he wouldn't tell him.

"He's been out all afternoon," Sid replied. "I expect him to be back for supper."

Rowry held back a snort. He could bet on that. Ord rarely missed a meal, but he was never around for the preparation of one, or the cleaning up. At times Rowry thought he would explode, but in deference to Sid's illness, he rarely said anything.

Ord came into the house just as Rowry finished putting the meal on the table. He greeted Sid, but he ignored Rowry completely. Rowry gritted his teeth.

"Have a good day, son?" Sid asked.

Ord was busy ladling food on his plate. He ate like a starved horse, and it always enraged Rowry to see Ord's indifference to anybody else. They were from the same parents, but they were as different as night and day. Ord was a selfish, churlish kid and Rowry doubted he would ever grow out of it. He sighed inwardly. He hated to think of what Ord would be like in a few more years.

"Have an interesting afternoon, son?" Sid asked.

"Interesting?" Ord threw back his head and brayed in coarse laughter. "Is there ever anything interesting in this town?"

He gulped down a couple more mouthfuls of food, then looked slyly at Rowry. "Mr. Big Man had an interesting afternoon though," he said and snickered.

Rowry stiffened. He knew that Ord must have heard about

Chubby Inman. He hadn't said anything about it to Sid for fear of upsetting him. He shook his head at Ord, and Ord ignored the signal. From this distance, he couldn't smell Ord's breath, but he was positive Ord had been drinking and hard. Ord's face was too flushed, and his eyes were glassy.

"Ord, what did he do that was so interesting?" Sid asked.

"He knocked the hell out of Chubby Inman. Split his head wide open with that damned rifle of his."

Rowry laid down his knife and fork, and his eyes burned. "You might as well tell him the rest of it," he growled.

Ord wasn't embarrassed at all. "Well, you did, didn't you?" he demanded.

"What did he do?" Sid asked.

"I split Inman's head open," Rowry snapped. "Inman was drunk and shooting up Brown's Saloon. He broke the front window and the backbar mirror. When his gun was empty, I knocked him unconscious. There were people in that room, but Inman was so drunk he didn't give a damn who he might hit. I dragged him to jail and locked him up."

"Inman's such a mild-mannered man," Sid said reproachfully. "Was it necessary to use so much force?"

"I thought it was," Rowry said heatedly. "It's part of my job." He stared at Ord, resentment bubbling up within him. This smart-mouthed kid had only brought it up to embarrass him with Sid. That seemed to be Ord's sole purpose in life; to make him look miserable before his father. Ord was grinning in open delight at Rowry's squirming.

"Did you have enough time from your drinking to learn all this?" Rowry growled.

That jolted Ord hard. He glanced quickly at Sid. "That's nothing but wild guesses," he said.

"All anybody has to do is to look at you and know what you've been doing. I suppose you were with those three cronies you usually hang around with."

Ord's face turned savage. "It's none of your business who I associate with," he snarled.

Rowry knew he had hit it right. Those three cronies were Verl

Wellman, the son of the town's biggest banker, Dent Edison and Chad Duncan. All three were about Ord's age, twenty years old, and they had hung around together since Ord was ten years old. Rowry didn't have any use for any of them. He considered all of them worthless. He doubted that the three had ever put in a solid day of work at anything.

"It is when you pick such scum," Rowry said. He pointed a finger at Ord. "Let me tell you this. Keep on running around with those three, and you'll come to a sorry end. Maybe even worse than Inman did."

Ord jumped to his feet, his face flaming. "You can't talk about my friends that way."

"I just did," Rowry said calmly.

For a moment, he thought Ord would charge him. If it hadn't been for Sid's presence, Rowry would have welcomed the opportunity to hammer some sense into the kid's thick head.

"I don't have to stay here and listen to you talk about my buddies like that," Ord raved. He whirled and tore out of the door.

"You shouldn't have talked to him like that," Sid said.

"He needed that, Pa," Rowry said firmly. "I wasn't just guessing. I keep getting reports of those four on some spree." He stopped, his face going harsh. Ord had never worked. Then where was he getting his drinking money? "Are you giving him money?" he shouted. He was so outraged he couldn't go on. If his guess was accurate, Sid was slipping Ord some of the money Rowry worked hard to get.

"What makes you say that?" Sid asked uneasily.

"There's only two ways he could get hold of any money," Rowry said heatedly. "He either got it from you, or he stole it. He sure as hell didn't work for it."

Sid breathed harder. "What if I do slip him a few dollars now and then? Is that a crime?"

Rowry was almost panting. "It is where Ord's concerned. We haven't got that kind of money for him to drink it away. Do you want him to wind up like Inman did this afternoon? He's pointed in the right direction."

Sid went into a hard coughing spell, and he looked weak when it was finished. "I'd better go lie down," he said.

Rowry sat there, still seething. Had Sid faked that spell, or was it the result of the heated discussion between them? Rowry didn't know, but he knew one thing for certain. He would be blamed for it. His appetite suddenly vanished, and he got up from his unfinished meal. Wearily, he set about clearing the table, putting the food away and washing the dishes. He was breathing harder when the chore was finished. This house was suddenly stifling; he had to get out of it.

He picked up his rifle where he'd leaned it in a corner and hurried out of the door. That damned Ord. He didn't know what he was going to do about him. He shook his head in utter disgust. He didn't know why he was so upset. Things had been the same for a long time. He lengthened his stride toward the office. Butler was on duty tonight, but maybe he would let Rowry take over, at least for part of the night.

CHAPTER 4

Butler looked up as Rowry entered the office. He whistled at Rowry's expression and demanded, "What happened? You look like a storm about ready to break."

Rowry smiled wearily as he sat down. "It's that damned Ord again. He never gives me a moment's peace."

Butler shook his head. "It's a bad thing when brothers differ, but sometimes it happens. Those kind of quarrels are the worst kind. What does your father say about it?"

Rowry threw up his hands. "He backs Ord in whatever he does. It's been that way since Ord was a toddler. Ma had a hard time birthing Ord, and she babied him. After she died, Sid took over, and he's got Ord spoiled so rotten that he smells."

"And you can't jump Sid because he's so sick?"

"That's about it," Rowry said wearily.

"You've got a tough row to hoe, Rowry. I can't see what you're going to do about it. Only wait until one or the other of them dies."

Rowry grimaced. "That makes for a pleasant picture."

"Can you see any practical solution?" Butler asked.

Rowry thought for a moment, then shook his head. "I guess not. That's why I had to get out of the house tonight. I couldn't breathe in there."

Butler shook his head in sympathy but didn't comment. He spent a few more minutes on some paperwork, then stood and reached for his gun belt. "Time for another round," he said. "Though I'll swear I can't see most of the times where it does any good."

"Let me make it for you, Creed," Rowry begged. "I need to stretch my legs."

Butler looked doubtfully at him, then nodded. "I can't say I'm unhappy with you for doing me a favor. My legs are killing me tonight." He thought for a moment, then said, "Rowry, don't let anything make you lose your head."

"Why would you say something like that?" Rowry asked. "Have I ever showed a streak like that before?"

"Never," Butler answered promptly. "But tonight falls under a different heading. I was thinking you might run across Ord somewhere in town. You've been chewing on a sour cud for a long time. Seeing him might push you into spitting it out."

Rowry grimaced at the dismal picture Butler painted. "It won't happen," he said flatly.

"You won't run across him, or you won't lose your head?" Butler persisted. "Which is it?"

"If I should run across him, and he ran off at the mouth again, I'd pass it up," Rowry said firmly. "I've got to keep Sid in mind, Creed. I can't do anything that might make him sicker."

"Good man," Butler said.

Rowry reached the door and turned. "I've got one thing to say. If I catch Ord breaking the law, I'll bust his butt as quick as I would anybody else's."

Butler chuckled. "I wouldn't expect anything different from you." He watched Rowry leave, and his face was sober. Rowry carried more of a burden than a man should. Butler didn't have the slightest idea how it would turn out, but he knew one thing for certain; Rowry had to be given some kind of relief, or he would break. He shook his head and went back to his paperwork. He paused before he started writing again, his eyes clouding. He knew Ord well—a smart, know-it-all, worthless kid. Butler wouldn't pick his kind to be his worst enemy. It was really amazing that Rowry had held his temper for as long as he had. The sickening part was that he couldn't do anything for Rowry; nobody could. Butler was kinless. At times he regretted having no one to love him. When that happened, all he had to do was look at Rowry and see how lucky he was.

Rowry walked slowly down the street. Most of the town's businesses closed early, and only the saloons showed patches of radiance before them. It suited Rowry just fine that the streets were so empty. In the mood he was in, he didn't want to be stopped by anybody.

The night was cloudy, and the feel of rain was in the air. Rowry wished a good downpour could wash away a man's troubles as it did the accumulation of surface debris. Stop thinking about Ord, he admonished himself. There were two things that could happen: Ord would grow out of his rotten ways, or somebody would put a bullet into him. Probably the latter, Rowry thought.

He turned onto Second Street, the street next to Main Street. It was even quieter than Main Street. Occasionally, he saw a light on in a house, but most of them were dark. The people of Hays usually turned in early to face the rigors of the next day.

He was passing the mouth of an alley when he thought he heard the scuffle of several feet. He started to turn, the hackles on his neck rising. He never completed the turn. Four dim figures came at him in a rush. The light was so poor, he couldn't get a clear look at them. Then they were on him, and the rifle was jerked out of his hand before his mind could adjust. "What the hell?" he said hotly. He didn't get another word out. Something crashed down on his head. From the force of the blow, he thought it was a club. If his hat hadn't absorbed most of the blow, he would have been knocked unconscious. He went down hard, his head rapping against the solid ground. All four of them were young and husky; Rowry could tell by the resiliency of their muscles. The second impact put bells to ringing in his head, and water flowed from his eyes. All of them tried to pile on him at once, and his dazed mind hampered his attempts to defend

himself. They rained blows on his unprotected face, and the fog-
giness grew worse. He was in close to them, and he made out a
startling detail. All of them were masked. It took Rowry a moment
to realize what they had on their faces, then he had it. Each one of
them was wearing a grain sack with holes cut out for eyes and
mouths. They had been drinking; he could smell the reeking breaths.
The ferocity of their attack was slowly wearing him down, and
Rowry attempted desperately to hold onto his senses. His head
roared, and his ability to think was slowly slipping away.

Another fist slammed him in the throat, and he gagged. They must
have been satisfied with the beating they had given him, for they
withdrew. He had the vague impression that, as they stood over him,
one of them said, "Maybe next time you won't make any smart
remarks about scum." Rowry heard a sharp, cracking noise of something hitting something solid, like a tree. His battered head wouldn't
let him make out exactly what the sound was. Something brutally
heavy smashed into his ribs, jerking a groan out of him.

That shoved him over the edge into unconsciousness, and he was
perfectly willing to just let go and slide into oblivion. He didn't hear
the four assailants leave.

Rowry had no idea how long he was unconscious. He came to
slowly, opening his eyes. The moment of lucidity didn't last long, for
he slipped away again. Each time he opened his eyes he entered a
world of pain, and he was just as happy to leave it again.

He came to again, and this time, with innate resistance, fought
against going under again. He tried to sit up and gasped under the
sharp, shooting pain in his ribs. Oh God! It hit him like the slash of a
saber blade, and his hand flew to the aching side. He didn't try to
press the injured area too hard. Gingerly, he felt the swollen spot and
guessed the pain came from a broken rib. That vicious kick had broken a rib and maybe even more. He lay back down, thinking about
the whole miserable incident. Those four didn't want to be seen or
known, or they wouldn't have put on those crude masks. The number
of attackers fit with what he was beginning to suspect. The only
words he had heard from one of them came back to him, and he
swore thickly. That one had said something about making a remark
about scum. Rowry had made a similar remark to Ord. There was

blood in his mouth, and it was choking him. Rowry spat it out. From the way the insides of his mouth hurt, one of those blows must have broken the inner flesh. His anger started then, burning like a clear, bright flame, and it helped sear away the pain. It lent him a crutch and helped him to get to his feet. Oh, it didn't kill all of the pain, for the only way he could keep from groaning was to keep his teeth clenched tightly. Each step took a heavy toll, but he managed to make it to the nearby tree, and he leaned against it. His head hung low and his vision wasn't good. He hung there until the fierce throbs of pain subsided. He could name those attackers, and he would do something about them. Not right now, he thought and grimaced. Right now all he could handle was getting back to the office.

He looked down, and his rifle lay on the ground in two parts. One of those punks had smashed it against this very tree, and the stock was broken away from the rest of the mechanism. That added new fuel to his anger, almost obliterating the hurt.

But the pain came back when he bent to retrieve the broken rifle. A sharp little yelp escaped him, and for an instant he thought he would black out. But he hung on until the fierce waves of pain lessened.

He was finally able to bend over far enough to clutch the ruined rifle. He was shaking all over when he straightened, and sweat ran off his face. Those four would pay for this. He didn't actually say the words aloud, but they rang in his head like a clarion bell.

By taking short, crippled steps and pausing after only ten or twelve of them, Rowry made his way back to the office. He was grateful he passed no one. He didn't want any of the townspeople to see him in this condition.

Butler heard him come in, and he whirled to watch Rowry's painful progress toward a chair. Until he reached it, Rowry wasn't sure he could make it. He lowered himself into it, careful not to arouse the savage beast that lay in his side. If he aroused it to action again, it would rip him to hell.

Butler's eyes were wide when Rowry finally sat down. "God, Rowry. What happened?" Rowry wasn't bleeding anymore, but the marks of bleeding were stamped on his face, and his shirt was bloody.

"I got jumped," Rowry said haltingly, pausing to garner enough strength to continue. "Four of them. They were masked. They came out of an alley before I knew it. They used a club or something and almost knocked me out. They worked me over good. For a little while, I thought they wanted to finish me. But that wasn't their purpose. They only wanted to beat the hell out of me. I tried to fight them off, but they had the surprise, and with their numbers—" He shrugged, and his voice trailed away. My God, he was so weak.

Butler cursed until he was red in the face. When he finally ran down, he asked, "Do you have any idea who they were?"

"I know who they were," Rowry said slowly. "They had grain sacks over their heads, and they'd cut out eye and mouth holes."

"Sounds like the work of kids," Butler observed.

"Not far removed from it," Rowry said. "My beloved brother was one of them."

Butler stared at him, astounded. "That's a rough accusation, Rowry. Are you sure?"

"I'm sure," Rowry said through gritted teeth. "We had an argument at suppertime. I was talking about Ord running around with that bunch of scum. One of them almost repeated my remark, and it wasn't Ord. Ord told them what I said. They got together and cooked up that attack."

"Name them," Butler said ferociously. "I just want to know their names."

"First, there's Ord," Rowry said. "The three he runs around with are Verl Wellman, Dent Edison and Chad Duncan."

Butler drew in such a sharp breath that it whistled. "You're sure it was banker Wellman's boy. The other two come from fairly good families, too."

"It was them," Rowry said firmly. "Those four have been running loose for a long time. That was what I was jawing Ord about. They think they've gotten real tough. They busted my rifle." He gestured at the weapon lying on the floor beside the chair. "The last thing one of them did was to kick me in the ribs. I think he busted a rib or two."

"I'll see that Doc Swanson gets here in a hurry. Then I'll pick up those four. I'll see how tough they are. Maybe some time locked up will convince them they're not nearly as tough as they think they are.

I'll go get Swanson. First—" He stopped, his eyes round in disbelief. "You don't want the doctor?"

"I want him all right," Rowry replied. "I don't want you going after those four."

"Why the hell not?" Butler asked belligerently. "They beat the hell out of my deputy. They bust up his rifle. If that's not enough to pick them up, I don't know what is."

"It's enough, Creed. But I'm thinking of Sid. It'd break him up to hear that Ord is arrested."

Butler swore again. "You mean you don't want those four punished because your Pa is sick? Rowry, that beating must have affected your brains."

Rowry wanted to laugh, but he couldn't. His mouth was too sore. "Oh, I'm going to see that they're punished. Before this is over I'll have Ord and the others squirming. I'll make them so damned fearful they'll be afraid to step outdoors for fear that the law is waiting for them." Butler was shaking his head again, and Rowry said, "Please, Creed. Let me handle it my way."

Butler stared at him a long moment, then gave in. "Well, all right. It was your beating. But I don't like it." He thought he had a telling point, and he demanded, "What about your rifle? Are you going to just let that pass?"

"I'm not letting anything pass," Rowry replied. His face contorted with pain. "Creed, will you get that doctor here for me? My side is beginning to give me hell."

"I'm going," Butler said ungraciously. "But I don't like it. God-damn it, it's like they beat me up when they jumped you."

"Please," Rowry said, holding out a hand.

"I'm going, I'm going," Butler grumbled. The door slammed behind him.

Rowry hoped to God it wouldn't take Swanson long to get there. That damned side was raising pure hell with him, and he didn't know how much longer he could stand it. He looked at the broken rifle and groaned. He didn't want Swanson seeing that, for it wouldn't fit with the story Rowry was already building in his mind.

He sucked in a deep breath, then gingerly rose. He bent over to pick up the rifle, and his face turned white. That had torn all the devils of hell loose in his side. His mouth opened, but he kept the yell of protest locked up in his throat. All he had to do was to find a new place for the rifle, then he could sit down again.

He had to lean on the desk for support as he worked his way around it. He reached the back side and tossed the rifle under it. It would take the most inquisitive of eyes to spot it.

He made it back to his chair and sat down, gasping for breath. Sweat had broken out all over him again. He didn't know how long he waited, but it seemed an eternity.

He opened his eyes as he heard the sound of footsteps at the door. Butler came in, followed by Swanson. Swanson was in his usual petulant mood, and he complained every step of the way. "What's this all about?" he protested. "It's getting so a man can't get a decent night's sleep."

Rowry forced a laugh, and it came out shaky. "All my fault, Doc. I was making the rounds, and I wasn't watching my step. You know that big old elm on Second Street?" He didn't wait for Swanson's nod. "I tripped over one of its roots and fell. I ran my face into the trunk before I fell. I landed on that damned root and think I busted a rib or worse."

Swanson's eyes narrowed as he studied Rowry's appearance. "It looks more like you were in a fight. Are you sure that isn't the real cause?"

Rowry gritted his teeth. "I told you how it happened. If you don't want to help me, Creed will find another doctor."

Swanson backed away before the severity of Rowry's attack. "Well, all right," he conceded. "If that's the way you want it. I'm afraid I'm going to have to cut your shirt away. It'd hurt you too much to try to take it off. Besides, you'd probably never get all the blood out of it."

Oh, goddamn it, Rowry thought. Would this old fool never get to work? "Cut away," he said weakly.

Swanson whistled as he bared Rowry's torso. "You really banged yourself up, didn't you?"

"That's what I told you," Rowry muttered.

"Your side's all enflamed," Swanson said. "Something's happened there. My examination may hurt." His fingers went to work, pressing against the swollen area.

Rowry gritted his teeth. Hurt? That was an understatement. Swanson's fingers were tearing him apart. My God, would this examination never end?

"Just as I suspected," Swanson said. "You've got a couple of broken ribs."

Rowry was sweating again, and the room swam before his eyes. "Can you do anything for it?"

"A little," Swanson said cautiously. "But the thing you need most is rest. You'll have to go to bed."

"For how long?"

"Three or four weeks," Swanson replied.

Rowry shook his head. "No way. I've got a job to do."

"You know you can take off all the time you need," Butler said heatedly.

Rowry flung him a fierce glance. He knew better than Butler what he had to do. "Doc, can you help it any?"

"I can wrap those ribs so that they won't tear you apart every time you move, but you'll still know they're there."

"Just get at it," Rowry said grimly.

"This is going to hurt," Swanson warned.

Rowry clamped his jaws tight. What in the hell did Swanson think he had gone through before? At Swanson's order he sat straight in the chair. Swanson started wrapping layers of bandage around his rib cage. Every turn made Rowry want to howl his head off, but he fought against yelling and managed to win.

Swanson finally finished the wrapping, and his face was sympathetic. "That can be as painful as anything a man has to go through. Does it feel any better?"

"I'll see," Rowry grunted. He drew a cautious breath and was surprised. The tearing, stabbing pain didn't come. "I think it feels better," he said cautiously.

"Good," Swanson said, pleased. "Now I'll have to patch up your face. This will hurt, too."

Rowry grunted. Maybe it would, but it wouldn't be anything like the pain he had suffered in his ribs.

the wounds, applied some salve to t
ey his work. "It may not feel any better,

y worked his jaw. Swanson was a pretty good d
ain had lessened to the point where he could forget ab
nuch do I owe you, Doc?"

ning," Butler said quickly. "You were hurt while you were or
The office pays for it."

Rowry looked at Butler's determined face, then gave up. He didn't
feel like arguing with Butler. He would only lose anyway.

"I'd better stop by your house in a couple of days," Swanson said, "and see if there's something else I can do for those ribs."

Rowry quickly shook his head. That wouldn't do. Swanson's appearance at his house would only tell Sid something was wrong. Rowry didn't want that. He also didn't want Ord to know that he suspected him and the other three. "I'll drop by your office, Doc."

Swanson's face clouded. He was getting ready to object.

"I can make it," Rowry said. "And I promise you I'll be careful."

Swanson had argued before with Rowry and had lost. "All right," he conceded. "You people sure are hardheaded. I'll be looking for you in a couple of days."

Rowry waited until Swanson left. "Do you think he suspected anything?"

"I'll bet he did," Butler replied. "Swanson's no dummy. Nobody would believe your story about falling."

"I don't give a damn whether they believe it or not," Rowry snapped. "That's the way it's going to be."

Butler sighed. "Swanson was right about one thing."

"What's that?" Rowry asked suspiciously.

"That you're hardheaded."

Rowry grinned sourly. "He said 'you people.' That includes both of us."

"I didn't get all banged up," Butler retorted. He stood, walked to the gun rack, unlocked it, and picked a rifle from it. He came back with it in his hands. "That's to replace the one you had smashed up."

"I can't do that," Rowry started to protest. He saw the determi-

Butler's face and stopped. "I can't tell you how gratef
d."

get it," Butler said brusquely. He walked over to the clos
ame back with a light jacket. "You'll need this to replace you
. Don't argue with me. Do you want people seeing all that band-
ing and asking nosy questions about it?"

"I sure wouldn't want that," Rowry admitted. He stood and
slipped into the jacket. His respect for Swanson grew. The movement
of getting into the jacket didn't tear him apart.

Butler had watched him anxiously. "How does it feel?"

Rowry grimaced. "I wouldn't want to live with it the rest of my
life," he admitted. "But like I told Doc, I'll live."

"Want me to take you home?"

Rowry's snort was answer enough. "The less Ord knows about
this, the happier I'll be."

"Rowry, you're not just going to let him off the hook, are you? He
deserves a lesson for what he did."

"He'll get it," Rowry said. "He'll look at me and wonder how
much I know. He's going to squirm."

"That's damned little payment," Butler growled.

"It'll be hard on him if he gets to thinking the law is watching
every move he makes. If you really want to help me, I want you to
dog every step those four take. Make them think they can't take a
breath without the law knowing it."

"I'll enjoy that," Butler said reflectively. "Those young smart
alecks will die a thousand times. We'll teach them a hard lesson,
Rowry."

"Intend to," Rowry said grimly. He picked up the rifle Butler had
given him. It was a good one, maybe as good as the one he had
wrecked. It felt good to be carrying it. He had carried a rifle for so
long he would feel naked without one.

He walked slowly to the door, turned there, and said, "Many
thanks, Creed."

"I didn't do anything," Butler growled.

"I think you did," Rowry said. "Good night, Creed."

CHAPTER 5

It took Rowry considerably longer than usual to walk home. The pain in his side wasn't nearly as bad as it had been earlier, but every now and then it grabbed him to let him know it was still there. He passed a half-dozen people on the way home, and every one commented on the jacket he was wearing. Some were jocular, others solicitous, but they added up to the same thing. "What's wrong, Rowry? You sick?"

He passed each remark over as lightly as he could, and he must have satisfied his questioners, for none of them commented further. He thought wryly that he had stamped out of the house to clear his head, and he wound up by having it addled. Your day's coming, Ord, he vowed silently. And the other three, too.

The house was dark when he arrived. He didn't expect Ord to be there, but he was concerned about Sid. He let himself in, walking softly, and listened at the door of Sid's bedroom. The regular snores coming from the darkened room relieved him. Sid had retired early. His breathing sounded as good as Rowry had ever heard it.

He made his way to his room, undressed carefully, not wanting to arouse that beast that seemed always to be just waiting. He crawled into bed, lowering himself with the utmost care. He could have sobbed with relief. He made it without bringing that stab of pain back to life.

He didn't have a comfortable night. He kept turning and twisting, trying to find a more comfortable position. If he turned wrong, that beast snarled and grabbed him. He looked drawn and hollow-eyed in the morning. He dressed and looked at his reflection in the mirror. You bastards, he thought, as he looked at the discolorations in his face. If anything, he thought his lacerations and cuts looked worse than they had last night. He dreaded facing the day. He couldn't hide all those marks, and inquisitive eyes were bound to pick them up. His face was too sore and tender to be shaved today. It would probably be several days before he even dared touch a razor to that poor, abused flesh. He sighed and went out to the kitchen to start breakfast. Using the utmost care and moving slowly, he could make it. He probably had a miserable day ahead of him. Oh hell, he'd probably have a lot of that kind of day ahead.

He had breakfast all ready when Sid came into the kitchen. Sid was bleary-eyed, and for a moment, he didn't notice the disfigurations on Rowry's face. "Best night's sleep I've had in a long time," he said with deep satisfaction.

"I'm glad to hear that, Pa."

Sid sat down at the table, and Rowry served him, keeping behind him all he could. Sid didn't get a full look at him until Rowry sat down across from him.

Sid's eyes widened in shock. He finally managed to say, "God Almighty, what the hell happened to you?"

"I tripped on a tree root last night while making a round of the town," Rowry said, keeping his eyes on his plate. "You know how a root will surface and crawl along the ground. My boot caught one of those. I fell and smashed my face against the tree trunk." He didn't say anything about the injured ribs.

Sid shook his head as though the story was too much for him to swallow. "You know what it looks like to me?"

"No, tell me."

"It looks like you got in a fight and took the worst of it."

"If I had been in a fight, why would I try to cover it up?"

"Beats me," Sid replied. "Unless you lost, and you're ashamed of it." He set to eating his breakfast, but the suspicion wasn't all out of him. Rowry could tell by the furtive glances Sid kept flinging his way.

"Say," Sid said, laying down his fork. "It just came to me. You and Ord were quarreling last night, and he stormed out of the house. You went out a little later. I heard you go. You went out to continue that quarrel with Ord. You got in a fight with him, and he marked you pretty good."

Sid's guess was pretty accurate; it just wasn't complete. "You can't believe that," Rowry scoffed. "You don't think Ord could do this to me?"

Sid stared at him, then shook his head. "I guess he couldn't. I still think you got in a fight."

"Oh, for God's sake," Rowry said wearily. "I told you what happened. Will you just skip it?"

Sid sat there, mumbling to himself. "If you didn't get in a fight with Ord, will you tell me where he is? He didn't come in last night. Not that I know of."

Rowry was just as happy he didn't have to look at Ord this morning. "How in the hell would I know?" Rowry flared. "Last night wouldn't be the first night he hasn't come home. You know that. He might not show up for two or three days."

"Why would he stay away from home that long?"

Rowry shook his head. He was sick of the whole subject. "Finish your breakfast, Pa."

Sid pushed his plate away. "I ain't hungry this morning," he said petulantly.

Rowry sighed. It wasn't going to be pleasant, spending the day here with Sid's suspicions picking at him. He might as well tell Sid about his time off. Maybe that would shut him up. "I'm not going to work for a couple of days, Pa." Maybe it would be even longer. It all depended on how fast he healed. But he'd always been a quick healer.

Sid's eyes clouded again. "You never took any time off before."

"This time I am," Rowry snapped. "Creed ordered me to take a few days off. He says he owes me."

Sid shook his head in disbelief. "I wish I knew what you're trying to hide."

"I'm not hiding anything," Rowry said testily. "If you're not going to eat, will you get away from the table and let me clear it?"

He washed and put away the dishes. Sid hadn't left the table, and Rowry could feel his eyes on him. He finished cleaning up the kitchen and said, "Pa, I'm going to lie down." He tried to grin and failed. "What good is time off if you don't take advantage of it?"

"All right, son," Sid said. "If you feel you can't trust your father."

"Oh hell—" Rowry walked to his bedroom and lay down. That beast in his side was trying to come to life this morning. All that stirring around hadn't done his ribs any good.

He'd managed to drop off into fitful slumber before Sid looked in and awakened him. "You sure you're all right, Rowry?"

Rowry sighed. He'd get damned little rest if Sid kept this up. "I'm fine, Pa," he said patiently. "Just trying to rest."

"I wish you'd tell me why you need it," Sid said.

"I don't need it," Rowry flared. "I'm just trying to take advantage of my day off." He turned carefully on his side, turning his back on Sid.

Sid stayed in the doorway a long moment, then moved away. Rowry turned back to his original position. He had been lying on the wrong side. He gritted his teeth until the beast crept away. If Sid kept up his solicitous behavior, it was going to be a hell of a day. Rowry had one thing in his favor. Ord wasn't here. It was small proof that Ord was guilty of taking part in the attack. Rowry had to be prepared mentally and physically to face him when he did come in.

Sid made two more trips to look in on him. Rowry pretended to sleep each time. It worked, for he heard Sid's long sigh as he left the doorway.

He did manage to fall asleep during the afternoon. He awakened near evennig, and he thought he was feeling a little better. He didn't try to push his luck, or that damned pain would grab him again.

He got up and set about preparing the evening meal. He didn't abandon his caution, but he'd be damned if he didn't feel better.

Sid picked at his food. "I wish Ord would get home," he said. "He worries me when he stays away. You sure you don't know where he is?"

"How many times do I have to tell you?" Rowry asked. "I want to see him, too."

That pacified Sid, and he finished his meal. Rowry thought about Ord's absence as he cleaned up after the meal. Ord's continued absence was only further proof that he was guilty.

"I'm turning in early, Pa," Rowry said as he started to leave the room.

Sid looked speculatively at him. "Damned funny you suddenly need all this rest. You're trying to hide something."

Rowry choked back his irritation. "I can't help what you believe. Good night, Pa."

"I'm going to wait until Ord comes home, Rowry."

You might wait all night, Rowry thought. He entered his room and undressed. He sure felt better. Not once did that piercing stab of pain cut through him.

He slept better the second night. He got up feeling refreshed. He was going to make it. Sid's expression at breakfast showed he hadn't had a good night.

"Ord didn't come in, Rowry." He sounded as though he blamed Rowry for that.

"I told you he might not," Rowry said. "I think I'd better go down and see if Creed needs me." He had to check with Doctor Swanson. He welcomed the excuse. Anything would be better than spending another day with Sid around to nag at him.

He stopped in at Swanson's office first. Swanson looked at him. "You look better than I expected. How do you feel?"

"Pretty good," Rowry replied.

Swanson unwrapped the bandages and caught Rowry's quick intake of breath. "Those ribs hurt with the support of that bandage gone?"

"And how," Rowry replied fervently.

"Don't move until I put on a new bandage." Swanson's probing fingers began exploring the tender spot. "I wouldn't have believed it if I hadn't seen it," he said incredulously.

"What's that?" Rowry asked.

"You didn't flinch as much as I thought you would. There doesn't seem to be much swelling, either."

Rowry grinned. "I'm a fast healer."

"You could be," Swanson said, but he shook his head. "More likely those ribs weren't broken as I first believed. They could be just cracked. Anyway, you're coming along fine." He wrapped new bandages around Rowry's torso.

"It's tighter than before," Rowry commented.

"I know. If you can stand it, it'll give you more support and cause you less pain." He waited until Rowry put on his shirt. "Move around a little and tell me how it feels."

Rowry took a cautious step, then another. His eyes widened. "Better, Doc. I'm beginning to believe you're a genius."

Swanson waved the compliment aside. "I learned a long time ago that every person is different. A lot of people would have been laid up for a long time with what you have. You're one of the lucky ones."

Rowry was beginning to believe that. "How much do I owe you?"

"I want to see you next week. Why don't I just put it on your bill?"

"Suits me, Doc, if it suits you." Rowry was beginning to have a higher opinion of Swanson. He wasn't the stubborn, crusty man he had thought him to be.

"Because you feel better doesn't mean you're to try to run a race," Swanson warned.

Rowry remembered the paralyzing pain he had had before. "No way," he assured him.

He went down the street, and he was happier than he had been a day ago. He could move with a minimum of pain.

Butler looked up as Rowry entered the office. "Goddamn it," he exploded. "I told you to take some time off."

Rowry grinned. "I did. I took off yesterday."

Butler shook his head in disgust. "You are one hardheaded man. Do you really feel better, Rowry?"

"I do," Rowry said earnestly. "Anything happen yesterday, Creed?"

Butler's face sobered. "Inman went up before a judge yesterday morning. The judge came down hard on him. He fined him a total of five hundred dollars. That included the fine and damages."

Rowry whistled. "He *did* come down hard on him."

"That's not all," Butler went on. "The judge gave him thirty days. I've got him locked up now."

"Christ," Rowry said softly. "What happens to his business?"

Butler shrugged. "I guess it stays locked up."

"Poor Chubby," Rowry said.

Butler nodded in solemn agreement. "It's nobody's fault but his own. He chose it. One good thing—he won't do any drinking while he's in here. Want to talk to him?"

Rowry shook his head. "Nothing I could say would cheer him up."

Butler's eyes darkened. "I never heard so much blubbering in my life. I could almost swear this little incident will convince Inman to stay away from the bottle."

"You think it will, Creed?"

"No," Butler said, shaking his head. "They never change. Some more interesting news for you. I ran into Ord and his three cronies early this morning. By the looks of them, they'd been out carousing all night. I chewed their tails off good. Maybe I had what happened to Inman on my mind. I told all four of them to get on home as fast as they could go. I promised the next time I caught them out on the town they'd regret it."

"Do you think you convinced them?"

"Hell no," Butler replied. "But maybe it scared them. You were right about them, Rowry. They're guilty as hell."

"Don't I know it. I'm going on home, Creed. I just checked with Swanson. He told me I'm getting along fine. He thinks it isn't as bad as he first thought. He rewrapped the ribs, and I can move better. Maybe I'll be back in the morning."

"You don't have to rush things," Butler said. "Take all the time you need. Use your head."

"I will," Rowry promised him. He left the office and returned home. Sid was up, and his face was jubilant. "You missed Ord coming home, Rowry," he said joyously. "He came home not more than an hour ago. He said he and the boys had been on a hunting trip. They didn't get back until this morning. He's gone to bed. You don't know how relieved I am to learn you two weren't fighting."

The goddamned liar, Rowry thought savagely. Ord had been out on a prolonged spree. He wished he could tell Sid that and make him believe it.

He spent the rest of the day lounging around the house. All Sid wanted to do was talk about Ord. Rowry knew he was going back to work tomorrow. He couldn't take much more of Sid's babbling.

He had the evening meal on the table when Ord walked into the kitchen. He looked at Rowry's battered appearance and malicious amusement shone in his eyes.

"You find something funny?" Rowry demanded.

Ord colored and gulped. "I didn't say anything."

"No, but you looked it," Rowry said savagely. He stabbed a finger at his younger brother. "Keep on the way you're going, and you're going to be one sorry smart aleck. Butler told me about running across you four this morning. Keep on the way you're going, and you're going to wind up in jail like Chubby Inman."

Ord looked sullenly at the floor. "You got no right to talk to me like that."

"Then I'm making it my right," Rowry said.

"What's going on between you two?" Sid wailed. "Can't we have one peaceful meal without you two bickering?"

"That depends on Ord," Rowry said calmly.

It certainly wasn't a peaceful meal. Ord ate sullenly, rarely lifting his eyes. Each time he did, Rowry's cold eyes were fixed on him. He knows I know, Rowry thought. Ord was already beginning to squirm. He had a lot more squirming ahead of him, Rowry thought.

Ord finished his hurried eating. "I'm going out, Pa," he muttered.

"You're not going to be out all night again?" Sid asked anxiously.

"He won't be if he's smart," Rowry replied.

Ord threw him a malicious glance and got up from the table.

"That boy worries me," Sid said after Ord left the house. "I don't know what's on his mind, but it's driving me wild."

"It will if you don't sit on him a little more."

Sid scowled at him. "You ain't helping matters any, always picking on him. Why don't you try to be more considerate?"

It was useless, Rowry knew. It was the damndest thing how humans got set one way and nothing could change them. He cleaned up the evening's dishes, then put on his hat. "I'm going over to see Abby."

"Both of you run out and leave me." Sid sounded on the verge of tears. "It's pure hell being old and sick. Nobody gives a damn."

Rowry wanted to yell at him but managed to hold his temper. Sid had it all wrong. The hell came from trying to get along with a stubborn old man and a willful brother.

He walked over to Abby's, and they sat on the porch. The moon came out from behind a bank of clouds, and Abby got her first good look at Rowry.

"Rowry," she gasped, "your face. What happened to it?"

"You've heard me complain about those three Ord runs around with?" At her nod, he went on. "They thought they were damned clever. They wore makeshift masks and jumped me a couple of nights ago. One of them used a club and almost knocked me out." He didn't tell her about his ribs. What he had already said was enough to worry her sick.

"How awful," she said. "You're sure?"

"I'm sure," he said grimly. "I said something about them before Ord went out that night. He didn't like it. He must have told them what I said, for one of them almost repeated the same words. They wanted to get even with me. They worked me over good."

"You should do something about it," she said indignantly.

"What would you suggest?" he asked wearily.

"If Creed knows about this, couldn't he arrest them?"

"He knows. I told him."

"Then why doesn't he do something?"

"Because I asked him not to." Rowry raised a hand to stop her outbreak. "You know how Sid feels about Ord. He thinks the sun rises and sets on that worthless pup. I've got enough on my hands without doing something that could make him feel worse."

They swung a few moments in silence. "But you can't just let it pass," she said.

"It won't pass," he said quietly. "Creed's already started rousting them around. He ran them off the streets this morning. After a while, those young punks won't think they're so smart. Every step they make will be watched. Between Creed and me, we'll make things so tough they'll have to reform or slink out of town." He paused for a moment, thinking. "The first isn't likely to happen. I'd settle for the second."

"Oh, Rowry," she cried. "They can be dangerous. Be careful."

"They've had the only crack they'll get at me."

He saw that his statement worried her, and he said softly, "I'll be careful, Abby."

"I wanted to hear you say that," she said and came into his arms.

CHAPTER 6

Rowry came back to work as he said he would. Butler was disgusted about it, but at Rowry's positive "I'm all right" gave up.

"Last night, I ran your four brave boys out of town again, Rowry. I found them in a saloon when I was making the rounds."

"Yes?" Rowry said, his eyes bright with interest. "What did you do?"

Butler grinned at a pleasant memory. "Evidently, they had just settled down to make an evening of it. I demanded to know where they'd gotten the money to spend in that saloon. All of them were indignant. I told them to furnish proof of getting that money honestly or get out." He chuckled. "That drove them wild. For an instant, I thought they'd try to be tough enough to jump me." He shook his head regretfully. "No such luck."

Rowry's eyes danced. "I wish I could have seen it."

"You probably will. They'll try it again. We can make Hays so hot for them, they'll try another town. That suits me all right."

Rowry thought about that solution. It would suit him, too. Maybe together the two of them could drive Ord and the others out of town. "I wonder how much pressure those four can stand," he said reflectively.

"We'll find out, won't we?" Butler asked. "Hell, this is giving me the biggest kick I've had in years. There's nothing I like better than going up against somebody who thinks he's tough."

Rowry strapped on his gun belt, and said calmly, "I told you I was coming back to work. I might as well get at it."

Butler opened his mouth to object, and Rowry said, "Creed, I wouldn't be fool enough to hurt myself now. I'll take it slow and easy. Why, it'll just be a walk about town."

"Don't forget to look for the terrible four."

"I won't," Rowry promised.

It took him longer than usual to make his round. An occasional twinge warned him the beast wasn't dead, just sleeping.

It was a pleasant morning, and he was happy to pause and exchange a few words with the familiar faces he passed. This would be a nice town and a good place to work if he and Butler could skim away the scum. They would, he vowed. It might take a little time, that was all.

He came back to the office and sat down with a sigh.

"See!" Butler said triumphantly. "I told you what would happen. You wore yourself out."

Rowry shook his head. "Not that bad, Creed. Just a little tired. That's all."

"Didn't I tell you you could take off until you were thoroughly healed? There's no need to punish yourself."

"How many times have you told me that, Creed? Fifty?"

"You don't lose any of that stubbornness, do you?"

Rowry grinned. "I try not to. That's part of my appeal."

Butler snorted in disgust. "Appeal, hell."

Butler was getting sore, and Rowry thought he'd better change the subject. "I didn't see any signs of Ord or his buddies."

"Maybe they've gotten the idea we mean business." At the objection forming in Rowry's face, Butler said, "It could happen. I've seen some tough men get the idea that a town doesn't want them. You wake up one morning and they're gone."

"I'd like to see that morning, Creed."

"It could happen," Butler repeated. "We're not dealing with men. They may be man-sized, but their brains ain't. Kids won't be nearly as hard to convince."

Rowry wished he could agree with him, but he couldn't. It wouldn't come that easy.

At the end of a couple of hours, Butler made a trip around town. "Rowry, why don't you take the rest of the day off?"

"Will you quit trying to baby me?"

"I forgot I was talking to the hardest-headed man in Hays."

"Just keep it in mind, and we'll get along just fine." Rowry's grin took the sting out of his words.

A week passed and each day was better. Rowry could almost swear that the beast that had been rampaging around in his side was dead. He hadn't known a twinge of pain the last couple of days. He had run across Ord and the other three a couple of times and had ordered them to get off the street.

"You can't do that," Ord howled.

"Don't you listen?" Rowry asked. "I just did."

The other three wouldn't look at him. They stared sullenly at the ground. This was Ord's brother. Let Ord try to reason with him.

"Why don't you quit jumping on our backs?" Ord whined. "We ain't doing nothing."

"That's the trouble," Rowry replied. "You haven't done anything all your lives. Get a job and start paying what it costs for your living. Then maybe I'll be convinced."

Ord tried to argue with him, and Rowry shut him up. "That's the way it's going to be, Ord. From now on. Creed feels the same way I do."

Ord's face was crimson. "You just wait and see," he snarled.

Rowry thrust his face forward. "What have you got in mind, Ord? You four want to jump me? Why don't you do it now? This would be a better time than the other one."

Ord went pale. He flashed a glance at the other three, and they had the same frightened expressions. "You got a lot of funny ideas," he said.

"Maybe," Rowry said complacently. "Now move. If you're sick of being rousted around, just split up. Go to work. That'd separate you four. I won't tell you again. Move."

He turned and started back for the office. He hadn't quite reached it when Henry Wellman came out of the building. Wellman looked as though he was sucking on a bad egg. Because Wellman was a banker, a lot of people looked up to him. Rowry didn't. Wellman couldn't even keep his own son in check.

"You ought to be damned proud of yourself," Wellman snarled.

That surprised Rowry. "What have I done?" He didn't like this man. He was long-faced as a horse, and there wasn't enough space between his eyes. Those eyes were as cold and unblinking as a snake's. He had only one goal in mind—to make as much money as he could. Rowry spat in the street. "If you've got something in mind, spit it out."

Those eyes fixed on Rowry's face. "There ought to be a law against ruining a good man," he said in his nasal tone.

"What in the hell are you talking about?" Rowry demanded.

"I just stopped by to talk to Inman. I had the unpleasant duty of telling him his note is due tomorrow. If he doesn't pay, I'll have to foreclose the note."

"That kills you, doesn't it?" Rowry asked mockingly. "Your biggest enjoyment is clamping down on people. You know Chubby can't meet that note. He's been in jail."

A flush washed across the dead white skin. "And you're the one who put him there. You're the one who ruined him."

Rowry's temper was seething. "Why, damn you." All pretense of being pleasant was gone from him. "You can't think I shouldn't have arrested him. That's my job."

"A useless one," Wellman said. "A man takes a few drinks, and somebody like you with misplaced authority slams him in jail. If people like you aren't checked, you'll wreck the entire town."

Rowry was so angry he could hardly speak. "You're pointing the wrong way, Wellman. It's people like you who can wreck the town. You'd never think of giving some poor, unlucky cuss a break. You'd never think to give him the little time he needs."

Wellman flushed, then paled. He was so furious that he quivered. "You can't talk to me like that," he shouted.

"I thought I just did," Rowry said mockingly.

"I'll tell you one thing. You'll be damned sorry you talked to me the way you did. I'll see this town doesn't want you. You just wait and see."

"Oh, shut up," Rowry said in disgust. He brushed past Wellman. He walked a dozen paces before he looked back. Wellman stood there as though his shoes were nailed to the ground. Rowry had never seen a man so angry.

He walked into the office and sat down. Butler took one look at him and said softly, "What happened to make you look like that?"

"I just had a run-in with Wellman," Rowry replied. "I can't get the taste out of my mouth. I lost my temper and said a few things, most of them having to do with how I feel about him."

Butler grinned. "I've only one piece of advice to give you. Don't ever try to borrow money from him."

"Small chance," Rowry scoffed.

"He was just in here, talking to Inman," Butler said.

"Did he tell you what it was about?"

"The bastard threatened to foreclose on Inman," Butler replied. "Can't you hear Inman?"

Rowry cocked his head and listened. A series of wails came from one of the cells, a rising and falling sound of despair. If Rowry had ever listened to a brokenhearted man, he was listening to one now.

"Poor Chubby," he said and shook his head.

"I'd stay away from him for a while," Butler advised.

Rowry looked astounded. "Why? I wasn't the one who foreclosed on him."

"No," Butler said seriously. "But he blames you for the whole thing. I tried to reason with him before you came in. He wouldn't listen. He claims if you hadn't arrested him, none of this would ever have happened."

"Holy Jesus," Rowry said. "Doesn't he blame himself?"

"His kind never do," Butler said dryly.

Rowry sat there frowning until Butler asked, "What's bothering you now?"

"I was just thinking," Rowry answered slowly, "there's so damned many odd people who crawl across the web a man builds for himself that the whole thing gets all tangled up."

"It's taken you this long to realize that?"

"I guess it has," Rowry said moodily. "You can add thick headedness to that stubbornness you accuse me of."

CHAPTER 7

There was a disbelieving look on Swanson's face as he finished his examination. "I've seen it, but I don't believe it."

Rowry grinned. "What don't you believe?"

"That you could be as close to being healed as you apparently are."

"I told you I was a fast healer."

Swanson smiled grudgingly. "Or I'm a better doctor than I thought I was."

"I'll give you all the credit," Rowry replied and laughed.

"It's been almost a month, hasn't it, since Butler came after me that night?"

"Lacks four days of being a month, Doc."

"It's still remarkable. Either you are a fast healer, or my diagnosis was sadly wrong." Swanson thumped his forefinger against the formerly tender area. "Does that hurt?"

Rowry shook his head. "I feel it, but I don't hurt."

Swanson used more force and thumped him again. "Feel that?"

Again Rowry shook his head.

"You know what that means?"

"You haven't told me yet," Rowry said.

"It means you won't have to come back. You're well."

That was good news. Rowry no longer had to be fearful of the beast coming to life again. He didn't have to have his ribs bandaged. With the weather growing hotter, those layers of material wrapped around him were uncomfortable. "What do I owe you, Doc?"

Swanson moved back to his desk, riffled through some papers, then said, "How does twenty dollars sound to you?"

"Fine," Rowry said, and paid up. He considered himself fortunate to get off as lightly as he had. Of course, paying doctor's bills wasn't his favorite way of spending money. That, too, would have to be chalked up to Ord and his three pals.

Swanson scribbled "Paid" across a bill and shoved it toward Rowry. "Wish all my patients were as prompt as you are. One small warning. Don't let those ribs take any more punishment for a while. Give them time to heal."

"I intend to," Rowry said with feeling. It wasn't likely that the incident would be repeated. He was more cautious now when he was around Ord and the others. They'd never take him by surprise again. He frowned slightly. He hadn't seen that bunch for the past week. He didn't think Butler had either, or else he hadn't said anything about it. Rowry wondered what Ord and his cronies were doing. Whatever it was, they were keeping it well hidden. He'd have to remember to speak to Butler about it.

He folded the receipt and stuck it in his pocket. "I'm obliged, Doc."

"Don't be," Swanson retorted. "You paid for everything."

"I still appreciate everything you did for me, Doc." Rowry waved to him and walked out of the office. What a relief it was to know that he wouldn't have to make any more visits to this office. As long as he was in the doctor's hands, it was sort of like being in jail for some minor infraction. He grinned as he thought that the best way to avoid a recurrence of that was not to get hurt or sick. He'd sure do his best to see that nothing like that happened to him.

He wandered uptown and saw a familiar pudgy figure less than a half block ahead of him. His face brightened. That was Dan Edmonds, the bank examiner. Edmonds was a much older man, and it was odd how their acquaintanceship had blossomed. They had met in a saloon, and over casual talk their interest in each other had grown. Ordinarily, Rowry wouldn't have any use for a bank examiner, and a bank examiner was as unlikely to ever need a lawman. But they had gotten to know each other well, and every time Edmonds was in town they used to spend a little time together. The time for Edmonds' regular visit had rolled around before Rowry knew it. He started to hail Edmonds, then held it. Besides being a little deaf, Edmonds was on the absentminded side. Probably his head was crammed with the figures he had just covered. If Edmonds had found something wrong with Wellman's books, nothing would give Rowry more pleasure.

He quickened his pace to catch up with Edmonds. The bank examiner wasn't aware that Rowry was anywhere near. His head was bent low, and he stepped off into the street to cross it. Rowry jerked his head around as he heard the clatter of hooves. Farther down the street, someone was screaming, "Runaway." Rowry's eyes widened as he caught sight of a horse pulling a buggy. It careened down the street. There was no driver. Rowry knew that bay mare. She was a skittish thing, and this wasn't the first time she had run away. Something had scared her into pulling on the reins tied to a hitch rack, and she was running free. Worse, she was headed straight for Edmonds, and he apparently didn't hear the clatter of those hooves.

Rowry judged the distance between the mare and Edmonds. There wasn't as much as he would have liked, but if he moved, he could make it to Edmonds. He broke into a hard run, cutting an angle, trying to save as much ground as he could. He didn't dare look behind him, but he knew that crazy mare was bearing down on them: the pound of her hooves sounded frighteningly loud. Both of them were in serious danger of being hit.

Rowry had almost reached Edmonds. There was no use trying to rouse him from his deep study. If he hadn't heard the horse coming, he certainly wouldn't hear Rowry's yell.

Rowry left his feet in a long dive, and his shoulder hit Edmonds at the waist. His momentum carried them a good two yards further before Edmonds fell. Rowry landed on top of him, and a worrisome thought flashed through his mind. Right after Swanson's warning to treat those ribs with care, here he was throwing himself like a wild kid.

He heard Edmonds' indignant splutter, and the horse dashed by them, the buggy careening from side to side.

"What the hell?"

Rowry rolled off him and sat up. His recklessness wasn't going to cost him; he didn't feel even a twinge. "Easy, Dan," he said. "I apologize for knocking you around, but you were right in that buggy's path."

Edmonds' eyes widened as he saw the disappearing buggy, and his face paled. "She would have run over me," he said wonderingly. "I didn't see nor hear her."

"I know, Dan," Rowry said soothingly. "But it's all over. Just be glad you weren't in her way."

"My God," Edmonds said, appalled. His hands were shaking as he brushed dust off his clothes. "You saved me from being run over. Hell, she could have broken some bones."

"But it didn't happen," Rowry said and grinned.

The owner of the horse and buggy pounded down the street. He stopped momentarily, breathing hard, his mouth opening and closing like a fish out of water. "She worked her tie loose again," he said unhappily. "She gets free, then she gets scared. Then she cuts out."

"You better break her better, Stark," Rowry said sharply. "Tie her more securely, or just shoot her. That crazy damned mare is going to hurt somebody real bad. What if a kid is caught in the street?"

"I know," Stark muttered, hanging his head. "I'll do something about her."

"Do that," Rowry said. His tone hadn't softened. Stark couldn't meet his eyes. He broke into a run again, yelling at the top of his lungs.

Rowry helped Edmonds to his feet. "You all right, Dan?"

Edmonds was still pale, but he nodded. "I think so, Rowry. I owe you something for this."

Rowry clapped him on the shoulder. "I'll think of something. Got time for a beer?"

"Can we make it later, Rowry? I'm late for an appointment with Wellman."

"Sure," Rowry said. He watched Edmonds trudge on down the street. He was a disheveled figure. But probably his ruffled dignity was the only damage he suffered. Rowry hoped so. He liked Edmonds.

He went back across the street and picked up the rifle he had dropped. He dusted it off and tried to blow away the remainder of the dust from the mechanism. It was a hell of a way to treat a good rifle.

Butler was in when Rowry walked into the office. "You look like you've been rolling in the dust," Butler stated.

"I have," Rowry replied. Briefly, he told Butler about knocking Edmonds down and out of the way of that wild mare. "Dan wasn't hurt, though he was shaken up some."

Butler nodded. "I imagine. Anybody would be if you came crashing into them." His eyes widened. "Did it do anything to you?"

"I thought of that," Rowry confessed. "I'd just come out of Swanson's office. He gave me a final check-over and released me. Wouldn't that have been a hell of a note if I'd busted something again?"

"We'd both die laughing over it," Butler said gruffly. "I'm going to have to talk to John Stark about his damned mare."

"I already did," Rowry said. "I think I scared him. He promised to be more careful."

"Promises ain't enough," Butler said savagely. The red was beginning to steal into his face, just as it always did when he was angry. "Do you know that's the third time this year that fool mare has broken away? I don't care if he has to shoot her."

Rowry grinned. "I told him just that." He sat down and began dismantling his rifle. "I dropped it in the dust when I dived at Edmonds," he said. "I want to be damned sure I get all the dust out of the working parts."

His fingers were busy for a moment, then he said, "That stupid mare tore through my web again."

It took a moment for Butler to catch what he meant, then his face cleared. "You still looking for the perfect conditions? Believe me, Rowry, they'll never happen."

"I guess not," Rowry grunted and removed the firing pin. He got a small can of oil from his desk drawer and, with a small piece of cloth, thoroughly oiled the pin. "But wouldn't it be nice if it could be that way?"

"It'll never happen," Butler said again. "Say!" he said as a thought occurred to him. "I haven't run across Ord and his friends for almost a week now. Do you think they've moved on?"

"I'd like to believe so," Rowry answered. He had the rifle parts laid out on the desk. He wiped off and oiled each part thoroughly before he went about the task of putting them all back together. "It'd make a nice world though."

"What would?" Butler asked absently.

"If you were able to remove everything that bothered you," Rowry answered.

"It'll never happen, Rowry."

Rowry sighed. "I guess not." He jerked his head in the direction of the cells. "Inman raise any more hell?"

"Not much," Butler answered. "I don't like the way he looks. Mostly, he just sits there silently. He's got a lot gnawing on his mind."

Rowry shrugged. "I'm sorry for him. But I can't do anything for him. He'll be off your hands in a few more days."

Butler nodded. "I'll be glad to get rid of him. He's been kinda stomping around in my web. You know, Rowry, I'm beginning to think like you. It'd be one hell of a world if all the annoyances could be removed."

Rowry chuckled. "Then you better go to work on it."

"What the hell do you think I've been trying to do all the years I've been wearing this badge?"

"You just haven't worked hard enough," Rowry said and laughed at the string of oaths issuing from Butler's mouth.

CHAPTER 8

The day Inman was released, Rowry came in late, as Butler requested. "I don't like the way Chubby's been talking," Butler had said to Rowry. "He's at the point where he's blaming the world for everything that's happened to him. No sense riling him up by letting him see you."

"Might be the wisest thing," Rowry had agreed. But he'd be damned if he'd spend the rest of his life trying to avoid Inman.

Rage and despair warred on Inman's face, making him look almost ludicrous. "You're the one who ruined my life," he blubbered. "You made me lose my business." He raised his free hand to dab at his eyes, and Rowry suspected he was wiping away tears. He felt pity for Inman but no sense of guilt. He had no feeling of responsibility.

"Chubby," he said reasonably. "You're blaming the wrong man. I didn't force you to drink. That was all your decision. Come on now, be sensible. Drop that gun."

Rage appeared in Inman's eyes. "The hell I will," he yelled. "You arrested me and took me to jail. You don't arrest other men for taking a few drinks." His voice rose to a triumphant note. "Why don't you arrest those other three at the end of the bar? They're drinking."

"But not enough to make them lose their heads," Rowry said patiently. "They don't get so drunk they shoot things up. They've learned to control their habit."

"You're saying I can't?" Inman asked in a brooding voice.

Rowry gestured with his free hand. "Judge for yourself, Chubby. You're back again, and you're carrying a gun. How long before you start blasting things again? I told you to drop the gun. I won't tell you again, Chubby."

"You think you're going to arrest me again?" Inman snarled.

"I know damned well I am," Rowry said quietly. "I won't tell you again."

"The hell you will," Inman thundered. "I ain't got any money to pay another fine."

Rowry debated his course for a moment. Should he keep Inman talking in the hope that all his spleen would be expended that way? How much pressure would Inman stand before he lost his restraint?

"Put down the gun, Chubby," he said. "Then we can talk this over."

"Because you tell me to?" Inman sneered.

Rowry saw the rage boil up into Inman's eyes. It told him that Inman had reached the breaking point. "Here now, Chubby," he said in a futile attempt to stall any action Inman had in mind. His words were too late.

"The hell I will," Inman screamed. "You're not putting me through that hell again."

He lifted the hand holding the gun, and Rowry could see it trembling as Inman tried to aim at him. He still wasn't convinced he couldn't talk Inman out of this foolish attempt, and he tried.

"Listen, Chubby," he pleaded.

The ancient gun roared. Rowry instinctively ducked. If Inman had been accurate, it wouldn't have done him any good. Nobody ducked a bullet. The bullet passed close enough to Rowry's head that he heard the wicked hum of its passage. He swung the rifle to hip level and pressed the trigger. He only wanted to wing Inman; a bullet would have to stop Inman where words had failed.

Rowry hadn't time for a well-aimed shot. He had raised the rifle muzzle and fired at almost the same time.

Inman grunted as the slug struck him. He coughed and straightened, and his eyes were reproachful as he stared a moment at Rowry. "Why, damn you," he said in a thick, slurred voice. "You took every—" His voice broke off, and he slumped to the floor.

The sickness rose in Rowry until he thought he was going to vomit. He could only see the profile of Inman's face, but he could see that a stream of blood was gushing from his mouth. Rowry didn't have to make a closer inspection to know what had happened. Instead of winging Inman, he had killed him.

The sickness came in waves. Rowry rested the muzzle of the rifle on the floor as a support for his trembling legs.

Brown had heard the shooting and rushed inside. One glance took in the whole sorry scene. "My God," he babbled. "You killed him."

"I didn't mean to," Rowry pleaded. "I was only trying to wing him. I didn't have enough time—" He broke off and briefly closed his eyes. He didn't have to explain this to Brown. He had witnesses in here who had seen everything. They would verify his story.

He opened his eyes, and they were hard with a peculiar brilliance. "Don't just stand there, Elmer. Go get Creed." His restraint broke and he screamed. "Goddamn it, move."

Brown cast him a frightened glance, then tore out through the swinging doors at a dead run.

For a long moment, there was an eerie silence, then the three customers broke their trance. They came toward Rowry, and he noted dully how their eyes avoided the body on the floor.

"Nothing else you could do, Rowry," Jim Beason said. "He shot at you first. I'm surprised you let him get off that shot."

Rowry felt as though he was in the middle of a nightmare. "I was only trying to nick him," he said in a lifeless voice. "Chubby and I have always been friends. I didn't want to kill him."

"Sure you didn't," Beason said softly. "But what the hell else could you do?"

The looks on the other two faces told Rowry that they agreed with Beason. It made things a little easier but not bearable.

He didn't know how long it took for Creed to come in. This awful nightmare was going to last forever. He turned his head slowly at the sound of heavy feet coming into the place.

At first, Butler didn't see Inman's huddled body on the floor. He said, "What is it, Rowry?" His eyes swung to the body, and his voice broke off. "Christ Almighty," he whispered. "Did you have to kill him?" That practiced first glance at Inman told him all. He had seen that ugly stamp of death often enough before to recognize instantly what had happened.

"I didn't want to kill him, Creed," Rowry said above the tightness that was choking off his voice. "But I had to." He had to stop; he was afraid he would choke.

The three customers approached Butler. Beason was the first to speak. "Rowry was trying to talk him into dropping his gun. Chubby was so crazed, it didn't look like he heard or understood what Rowry was saying."

The other two nodded solemnly. "Rowry gave him a chance. A chance most men wouldn't have given him."

Butler's narrowed eyes evaluated Rowry's expression. "Get on back to the office, Rowry," he said, his face stern. "I'll take care of things here."

Rowry nodded dully, tucked the rifle under his arm, and stumbled blindly out of the room.

He walked back to the office with unseeing eyes. All the better times he had known Inman flashed through his mind. The bad times seemed to be fading into nonexistence. He entered the office and sank into a chair.

Butler came in a half hour later. He looked searchingly at Rowry and asked, "The first one you've killed, Rowry?"

Rowry nodded without speaking. Reaction was setting in, racking him cruelly. "I didn't want to, Creed," he said hollowly. "But he got off a shot. I swear its air touched me. I tried a snap shot, but there wasn't enough time. I didn't want to—" His voice kept rising on him, and he choked back the remainder of the sentence.

"Stop it," Butler snapped. "You gave him more chance than he deserved. I don't know of another law officer who would have waited that long. Everybody who saw it verifies your version, Rowry. It was just one of those things that couldn't be avoided."

Rowry's eyes were stinging, and he ducked his head so that Butler couldn't see his eyes. "I'm glad to hear you say that," he said haltingly.

Butler was pacing back and forth. He stopped and leveled a finger at Rowry. "Let me tell you one thing. You pulled a damfool stunt. You had every reason to suspect that Inman was unsettled. You got away with what you did this time. Don't ever try to pull it again, or I'll be burying a deputy."

Rowry coughed. "I keep thinking of the way things were and how much better it would be if they could be turned back."

"Oh, for God's sake," Butler snorted. "You're determined to punish yourself, aren't you? Chubby was dead set on a course. You used the only thing that could have turned him."

Rowry worked his jaw. Butler's words were helping. "Creed, do you remember the first man you shot?"

"I remember every damned one of them," Butler said roughly. "It's something you can't get out of your head."

"But you just kept on," Rowry said.

"I had to if I wanted to keep my badge," Butler said. "It was as simple as that."

Was there some kind of warning in those words? Rowry thought about them and decided not. Butler was only trying to be helpful. "You stayed at Brown's a long time, Creed."

"Only until Simmons came and took Inman away. Chubby's being buried tomorrow." His face toughened as he caught the flash in Rowry's eyes and guessed what he was thinking. "Don't have any fool plans to go to that burial. It wouldn't do you or Inman any good."

Rowry's sigh was a long, tearing sound. So this was the way a man turned his back on an unpleasant situation; he simply didn't show up.

"So that's the way it ends," he said, a tinge of bitterness in his voice.

"You won't be that lucky," Butler said with brutal candor. "Mayor Reaves will demand a full investigation. He's pretty touchy when something like this happens."

Oh damn, Rowry mourned silently. He'd have to relive this nightmare again; he would have to relate every word, every action.

Butler had been studying his face. "Now what the hell are you thinking of?"

"I was just thinking that Chubby really tore my web to pieces," Rowry answered slowly.

"It'll only be a formality," Butler said impatiently. "Oh, come on, Rowry. Think of how lucky you are. Suppose there were no witnesses willing and ready to testify in your favor."

Rowry tried to smile. It hardly cracked the stiff facade of his face. At least Butler wasn't displeased with him. That was something to cling to.

CHAPTER 9

Rowry spent a restless night. Sleep could be the stubbornest thing in the world. When a man needed it desperately, it wouldn't come. All he could think about was that investigation tomorrow and its outcome.

Maybe he got a couple of hours of sleep. He grabbed a couple of slices of bread, and that would have to do him until he reached town. He slipped out of the house just after dawn.

He walked downtown, and Ma Atkins' restaurant was open. There wasn't another restaurant in town that kept such murderous hours.

Those hours must have been profitable, or she wouldn't have kept them.

Two men were at the counter, and Rowry took a table to avoid talking to them.

Ma Atkins saw him, came around the end of the counter, and walked over to his table. "Morning, Rowry. What can I do for you?"

She was a plump, homely woman, and the long hours had taken their toll of her. Her husband had died a dozen years ago, but Ma had never wasted any time bewailing her plight. She just pitched in and made herself a living. She was a tough old girl; she was a survivor.

Rowry ate in here every now and then, and he was no stranger to her. He wondered if her eyes rested longer on his face than usual. Surely she had heard about Inman's shooting. If she had any untoward thoughts about the shooting, nothing showed in her eyes.

"Morning, Ma," Rowry returned. "I'll just have scrambled eggs and coffee."

"Sure that'll be enough to hold you?" she asked.

What did she mean by that? Was she saying that wasn't enough food to sustain him for the ordeal that lay ahead of him? "It'll do, Ma," he said flatly.

She had the eggs and coffee ready in a few moments.

Rowry tasted his coffee. It was piping hot and good. The eggs were the same. She had built herself a reputation by the tastiness of the food she served.

"It's just fine, Ma," he assured her.

"I'm glad," she said softly.

He wished he could read the thoughts behind her eyes. Did they hold pity or censure for his actions of yesterday? He sighed and broke off his thoughts.

The two men at the counter twisted their heads around and took a long look at him. They exchanged knowing looks and Rowry heard the murmur of their talk. He couldn't hear the words, but his face burned just the same. He could bet that the talk was about him. A brief snicker from the men confirmed his feeling.

He put the two men out of his mind. They could say whatever they pleased about him. He could feel the heat of his anger stealing up his neck, but violent protest against a private conversation wouldn't do him any good before the investigation.

The two men finished their breakfast before Rowry was halfway through eating. He heard them coming and lowered his head over his plate. Maybe they would pass by without comment. God, he hoped so.

"Well, Bill, would you look who's eating with us?"

"Nothing surprises me, Hump. His kind have got the gall to show their faces anywhere."

Rowry breathed hard, and he could feel his ears getting hotter. He knew both of those voices, and he knew what they were referring to. He stubbornly kept his head down.

Both of them stopped by his table. "Shoot anybody else today, Deputy?" The nasty question was followed by another snicker.

Rowry could stand it no longer. He jerked his head around and glared at Bill Slavins and Hump Bevins. Both of them had been cast in the same rough-cut mold, and they were potential troublemakers. Hump was a huge man with broad shoulders. His neck was practically nonexistent, and the lack of it threw his head forward, making him look as though he carried a hump on his back. A broad grin was plastered all over his broad, red face.

"That's none of your goddamned business," Rowry snapped.

The grin was wiped off Hump's face. "The hell it ain't," he said in an offensive tone. "When one of our law officials goes around shooting innocent citizens, it's time that some of us objected."

That tore it wide open for Rowry, and his hands itched to get at them. He didn't give a damn how bad it would look at the investigation. No lowlife could talk to him like that.

Before he could make a move, Ma came around the counter, her short legs pumping hard. Her face was suffused with anger as she put herself between Rowry and the other two. "That's enough," she roared. She had a voice as deep as any man's, and her anger gave it power.

"Hell, Ma," Hump protested. "You can't say you approve of what this deputy did yesterday?"

"I know all about it," she said grimly. "He did what he had to. In my opinion, he shot the wrong man. He should have started in here.

No loudmouth is going to criticize him for doing his job. Now clear out of here."

Hump's jaw dropped. "You mean you're turning against good paying customers?"

"I sure as hell am." She bit off each word. "Don't pride yourself on being good pay. I've got a bill against you two that's getting age on it. Get out of here. I don't need or want your kind of business. Don't ever come back in here again."

That tough, dumpy little figure of a woman with its face set belligerently whipped all the inclination to argue out of those two.

"Come on, Hump," Slavins said. "This place was getting on my nerves. It'll be a pleasure to avoid it from now on."

Both of them tried to regain some of their aplomb as they sauntered out.

"Scum," Ma said, and Rowry thought she was going to spit on the floor.

"Ma, you didn't have to do that," Rowry said, distressed. "That cost you paying customers."

"Those two? Hah! The sooner I get rid of those kind, the better off I'll be."

The distress didn't leave Rowry's face. "You can't stop people from talking about what happens in town, particularly if it's exciting and bloody."

"Maybe not," she said, the grimness still in her voice. "But I sure as hell can pick out who eats in here. You're going to run up against a lot of that, Rowry."

"What's that, Ma?"

"People's loose, wagging tongues. The less they know what really happened, the more those tongues will wag. They make me sick. I knew Chubby Inman pretty well. He ate in here a lot. Nicest, most pleasant man you'd ever want to know. But when he got some of the juice in him, that was a different matter. He was downright mean and ugly. I've had to order him out of here a couple of times. Do you know, I thought he was going to try to knock my head off?" Her jaw jutted. "He'd have been the sorriest male in the world if he had tried something like that. The minute I could get my hands on something,

I'd have split his head wide open. Maybe people just remember the pleasant Chubby. I remember the nasty times."

Rowry smiled slowly. "Thank you, Ma. You don't know how much I appreciate that."

"Pshaw." She made a slash through the air with the edge of her palm. "Don't you worry none about the investigation."

Rowry's eyebrows rose in surprise. "Do you know about that?"

"Shucks, everybody in town does. That's all they talked about during supper last night. Some of them said you were going to catch hell and be fired. Others argued just as fierce that shooting him was the only thing you could do." She looked at his unfinished eggs. "Here we stand gabbling, and your food's gotten cold. I'll have some hot eggs in just a moment."

"It was as much my fault as yours," Rowry objected.

"If you don't let me get you some fresh food, I'll always believe it was because I pushed in where I didn't belong."

Rowry smiled. "I wouldn't want that for the world, Ma."

She was gone perhaps a little longer this time, and Rowry looked at the generous portion of ham she had added to his order. "You can't do that, Ma," he protested.

"It's my place, ain't it? I can do anything I want. Besides, I think you're going to need something substantial to bolster you. Don't let any of those snotty noses run over you."

For the first time in several hours, Rowry felt like grinning. "Ma, I can't tell you how much I appreciate you."

She ducked her head. "Then don't try," she said tartly. "Go on. Eat that while it's hot." She turned and waddled away.

He watched her with warmth, then fell to eating his breakfast. A little while ago he hadn't had much of an appetite, but now he was as hungry as a wolf.

He finished the meal and walked up to the counter, reaching into his pocket as he did. He started to withdraw his hand, and Ma was shaking her head.

"This one is on the house, Rowry," she said. "Damn it, it's one little way to tell you how glad I am that you're here to protect me."

He withdrew his hand empty. He leaned over the counter, seized her face in both hands, and pulled her head toward him. He kissed her soundly on the forehead.

She was blushing when he released her. "What was that for?"

"Maybe I had to show a little appreciation, too, Ma."

"I swear the younger generation hasn't got an ounce of brains in their head. Will you get out of here and let me get at my work?"

"Thanks again, Ma," he said and strolled toward the door. He looked back from there, and her eyes were fastened on him. They were all squinched up as though she was trying to hold back tears. He blew her a kiss, and she doubled up a fist and shook it at him.

Rowry walked toward the office. He could swear the sun was shining brighter. All his worries about the coming investigation seemed to have vanished.

He unlocked the office door and entered. He didn't expect Butler to be down this early. He was slouched in his chair, his bootheels hooked over the edge of the desk when Butler finally came in.

"What are you trying to prove?" Butler demanded. "That you're a hard worker getting on the job early? You don't have to; you've already got the job." A grin softened the crustiness of his words. He settled down, and those perceptive eyes ran over Rowry's face. "A rough night, Rowry?"

"It was. But breakfast wiped all the stewing and fretting away."

"How's that?"

Rowry related the incident at Ma Atkins' restaurant. "I swear I was about ready to tear into those two big mouths. Before I could make a move, Ma Atkins ripped into them. She tongue-whipped them good. Then she fixed me another breakfast to take the place of the one getting cold. She not only wouldn't listen to me, she refused to take any payment."

"She kinda put your web back together again," Butler said.

Rowry nodded. Just the memory of the incident put a lump in his throat.

"She's damned good people," Butler observed. "I've been trying to tell you for a long time that most people are sound. But you kept your attention fixed on the loudmouths. It makes you feel good, doesn't it?"

"It sure does," Rowry said emphatically.

"Maybe it'll put you in a better frame of mind for the hearing," Butler said.

Something in his tone caught Rowry's attention. "Do you expect it to be a rough one?"

"No more than usual," Butler answered quickly. "Mayor Reaves will be there, and Judge Chambers will conduct it. And Joe Kearns," he added. His face looked as though he had bitten into something bad.

Kearns was the town's prosecuting attorney. He was a small, dapper man with a weasel-like face. He had a sharp mind, and he bored in. Rowry wondered why Kearns kept his job. He rasped most people he came in contact with. Rowry knew Butler didn't like him. There had been several clashes in the past when Kearns had tried to prove that the marshal was in the wrong. Some heated words had passed between them.

"Sounds like a regular trial," Rowry observed.

"That's what it'll be," Butler said. "Now don't get to stewing. It's always like that in matters like this. You ought to be glad. This investigation will squash all doubts for good. We've got to leave a little before ten."

Rowry nodded. The worries were returning, nibbling at him with those little rat teeth. He didn't realize Butler was watching him until Butler said sharply, "Stop it."

"Stop what?" Rowry asked in surprise.

"That stewing. It shows on your face."

"I guess it does," Rowry admitted. "Creed, were you ever through one of these things?"

"Several times," Butler replied. "The ordinary man is frightened of the man who carries a gun and has the authority to use it. So they try to tear him down every chance they get. I told you, all the witnesses are on your side. You're lucky in that respect. A couple of times, I didn't have favorable witnesses. Judge Chambers is a fair man. Get your mind off it. Think about something else."

Rowry couldn't promise he would, but he could try. He thought of Sid and Ord and Abby. Then people like Hump and Bill Slavins crept into his thoughts. Then he'd think about Ma Atkins, and the sharp rat teeth withdrew.

The time passed slowly until Butler said, "Time to go."

Rowry nodded and stood. "Guess I don't need this." He walked over and deposited the rifle in the gun rack.

Butler grinned savagely. "Good thinking. Don't want to frighten the little men." He unbuckled his gun belt and laid it on his desk.

They walked out, and Butler locked the door behind them. "Where are those peaceful days that I used to think were too dull?" he asked.

"I don't know," Rowry replied. "But I'd sure like to get them back in a hurry."

"Two of us," Butler said and grinned fleetingly.

They hadn't gone a half block toward the courthouse when Wellman came toward them. "Ignore anything he might say," Butler hissed. "Don't let him rile you."

Wellman stopped in the middle of the walk, and Butler and Rowry started to go around him.

"Just a minute," Wellman said importantly. "I want to talk to Rowry."

"He doesn't want to talk to you," Butler said brusquely. "We don't want to be late for our appointment."

"You better not be," Wellman said and sneered. "It could be the final proof that the investigating board needs in order to see how incompetent an officer you are."

Rowry didn't get a chance to speak. Butler's sharp motion cut him off before he could get a heated word out of his mouth.

Butler moved a step forward and thrust his face into Wellman's. "What's that supposed to mean, Wellman?"

The tone of Butler's voice was an affront, and Wellman colored. "Don't tell me you still back him up after he killed an innocent man?"

"You shut your damned mouth," Butler thundered. "Rowry shot a drunken, crazed man, a man who was trying to shoot him."

"His story," Wellman sneered.

Butler was thoroughly angry. "A story that four witnesses back up. Wellman, I'll give you some sound advice. I wouldn't stick my big nose into something you know nothing about. It could kick back on you one of these days."

He brushed roughly by Wellman, and Rowry followed him. "Get that look off your face," Butler stormed. "I heard what Wellman said. It doesn't matter a damned bit what he thinks. He's got nothing to do with this investigation. You're not going into that hearing looking like you're sore at the world."

Rowry forced himself to cool down. As usual, Butler was right. "You said there were four witnesses, Creed. There were only three."

"You're leaving out Brown."

"He didn't see it," Rowry insisted stubbornly. "He stayed outside."

"Yes, but he suspected what could happen," Butler argued. "He knew the mood Inman was working himself into."

"I wonder why Wellman interfered," Rowry mused. "I never did anything to cross him."

"Maybe you have," Butler said reflectively. "Maybe that snot-nosed kid of his told him about us rousting Ord and the others around."

Rowry's face cleared. Butler had probably hit on the answer. "I think you've got it, Creed."

Butler hawked and spat in the street. "Sure I'm right," he said. "By rousting his precious boy around, you walked on Wellman's tender corn. Your big trouble is that you let the freaks in this life get at you."

Rowry couldn't argue with that reasoning. "Just tell me one thing, Creed. How do you avoid them?"

Butler grinned at him. "I haven't lived long enough to figure that out."

They walked into the courthouse together. Quite a few people were waiting for them. Rowry was just grateful that this hearing wasn't open to the public. Judge Chambers nodded at him. Mayor Reaves and Joe Kearns sat together, their heads close. There were the three customers who had witnessed the incident, and Elmer Brown. Rowry was surprised to see Jeff Kilarny present.

Butler noticed his surprise and explained, "Kilarny is a good man to bandy words with Kearns. He's crossed swords with Kearns before. And usually won. He's one smart lawyer. In a matter like this, I think it's smart to have a lawyer to protect you."

"All right," Rowry agreed. "If you think it's necessary."

"I do. Kearns and Reaves run around together too much to suit me. Kilarny will pull their fangs."

Rowry sighed as he sat down. This was becoming a lot stickier than he had imagined.

Kearns stood and adjusted his coat lapels. He reminded Rowry of a banty rooster preening his feathers. "I think we can begin, Your Honor," he said. He had an orator's tongue, smooth and oily. "We're here to decide a serious matter, the shooting of an innocent man by a law officer without any provocation."

Kilarny jumped to his feet. "Objection, Your Honor. We haven't heard all the witnesses. It's too early to reach such a conclusion."

Chambers nodded. "Sustained. Mr. Kearns is always prone to rush matters."

Kilarny winked at Rowry as he retook his chair. Kearns sat down, his face sulky.

"Proceed, Mr. Kilarny," Chambers instructed.

Kilarny had a tough Irish face. He enjoyed a rough meeting of minds, and he was adept at protecting himself. "Marshal Butler," he said.

Butler took the witness chair.

This was going to be handled like any ordinary criminal trial, Rowry worried. Maybe for the first time, he realized how serious this could be. It could turn against him.

"Will you tell us your part in this unfortunate incident?" Kilarny asked.

Butler cleared his throat. "I was called in after the shooting," he stated. "It was all over when I arrived. Inman lay dead on the floor. Rowry looked bad."

"How do you mean, bad?" Kilarny asked.

"You know, sort of a green look about the gills. As though he was going to be ill. It was the first occasion Deputy Saxton was involved in something as final as this was. Rowry was bad shook."

"He should have been," Kearns said waspishly. "Shooting an innocent man."

"Objection," Kilarny screamed.

Chambers pointed a finger at Kearns. "I won't warn you again.

Another outbreak like that, and it'll cost you dearly. Go on, Marshal."

"I took over," Butler said. "I took care of the arrangements for the burial of the body."

"Is that all you know about this?" Kilarny asked.

"No, sir. Inman started going to pieces shortly after banker Wellman visited him in his cell. Inman was doing thirty days after his last drunken spree, when he shot hell out of Elmer's saloon. Wellman had a note of Inman's coming due, and he foreclosed on him. There was no way Inman could meet that note, penned up in jail like he was. I think his mind began to slip then."

"Is this your guess, Marshal?" Kilarny questioned.

"Maybe about his mind slipping," Butler admitted. "But he had enough cause. He knew he was going to lose his business. I knew about the foreclosure. I took Wellman back to Inman's cell, and I listened. Inman begged for more time, and Wellman turned a deaf ear on him. From that moment, Inman started going. He talked a lot to himself, and some of it was wild. He kept saying he'd get the man responsible for all his trouble. In his twisted mind, he centered all his dislike on Rowry. You know Rowry arrested him for drunkenness the first time. I remember the day Rowry dragged him to jail. That little spree cost Inman thirty days in jail and a heavy fine."

Kilarny leaned forward, his face intent. "How long did Inman keep up this odd behavior?"

"Almost all the time he was locked up," Butler replied. "I tried to reason with him a couple of times. I pointed out that he should be sore at Wellman. Wellman foreclosed on him, not Rowry."

"How did he take that advice, Marshal?"

"He didn't take it at all. He kept insisting that if Rowry hadn't arrested him, he wouldn't be in jail and he could have made that note. He was still swearing about his fancied abuse the day his time was up."

"Is that all you know about it, Marshal?"

"That about ties it all up. Except that I warned Rowry to stay clear of him for a few days. Give Inman enough time for his head to settle down."

Kilarny nodded. "Dismissed. Your witness, Counselor."

Kearns looked at Butler a long moment before he shook his head. He had had too many run-ins with Butler, and he still bore the scars of them. "No questions," he said.

Rowry stood as his name was called. His palms were wet, and he felt sticky all over. A lot of his future depended upon how well Judge Chambers believed him. Butler had told him on the way here, "Just tell it like it happened. Don't try to get fancy and dress it up."

"We'd like to hear your account, Deputy," Kilarny said.

"I was making a round of the town. Elmer Brown came running down the street toward me. He was out of breath and so scared he could hardly speak. Inman was in his saloon, drunk again. Worse, he was holding a pistol."

Kilarny's eyebrows rose. "Drunk *again?* Did this happen often?"

"Yes, sir. I had arrested him several times for the same offense. Brown said Inman brought a bottle in with him, and it was half empty already. Inman kept muttering he was going to get even with the man who caused all his trouble."

"Meaning Mr. Wellman?"

Rowry shook his head. "He meant me. Brown told me he said my name a couple of times," Rowry answered.

Kilarny looked incredulously at him. "Knowing all this, you went into that saloon anyway? Why didn't you turn it over to Marshal Butler?"

Rowry shook his head in that slow, determined gesture. "Inman wasn't looking for Creed. He was looking for me. I had to go in. It was part of my job."

"You were either a brave or a foolish man, Deputy," Kilarny murmured.

"I didn't stop to think much about that," Rowry said. "A drunk was on the loose and armed with a pistol. I had to try and get the gun away from him."

"Go on," Kilarny said.

Rowry licked his lips before he continued. He had the attention of everyone in the room. Even the judge was leaning forward intently. "I told Brown to wait outside until I got the gun away from Inman. I went through the doors, and only three other customers were in the room." He nodded in the direction of the three witnesses. "They're sitting over there." He paused for a moment, picking through his thoughts. He wanted to tell it exactly as it happened. "I moved in on Chubby slow. I called to him and asked him to drop the gun. He was so drunk he was slow and clumsy. He almost tripped over his own feet. He cussed me out good and swore he was going to shoot me for bringing all this trouble down on him. He swung the gun up and fired at me."

"Was your rifle trained on him?" Kilarny interrupted.

Rowry shook his head. "It was pointed at the floor. I didn't think it would come to that point."

Kilarny nodded. "Proceed."

"I heard the bullet pass right by my head. Before he could fire again, I swung my rifle barrel up and fired a shot, hoping to wing him." He shook his head, his eyes blank and staring as he relived that scene. "Everything was happening too fast. I didn't have time to be too choosy in my aim. I fired and Inman went down." God, his mouth was dry. He ran his tongue around his mouth, trying to work up a little saliva. "I didn't wing him," he said simply. "I hit him dead center." He slumped in his chair. Telling all this had exhausted him.

"Your witness, Mr. Kearns," Kilarny said.

Kearns advanced briskly toward Rowry. There was a sort of eagerness in his eyes, and it gave him a hungry look. "Did you know Chubby Inman well, Deputy?"

"Very well. I've eaten a few meals with him, and I've had several beers with him."

"Was he a quarrelsome man?"

Rowry shook his head. "I'd say the opposite. He had a deep, booming laugh, and he couldn't go long without it ringing out."

"Did you consider him a friend?"

"I did," Rowry answered.

Kearns threw up his hands in horror. "You'd kill a good-natured man, a man you called a friend, with no reason?"

Rowry felt his cheeks burn. "I told you how and why that happened," he snapped.

"But you went ahead and shot him down," Kearns persisted.

Kilarny was on his feet, bellowing. "Your Honor—"

Chambers cut him short. "I understand, Mr. Kilarny. Mr. Kearns,

I think it's been well established why the shooting was necessary. There's no reason to chew on it like a dog with a bone."

"But, Your Honor," Kearns protested. "I was only trying to establish my case."

"And you're only succeeding in wearing out the judge," Chambers said wearily. "If you haven't any more pertinent questions, I suggest you dismiss the witness."

Kearns threw him a resentful look, but he said in an unhappy voice, "No more questions." There was a noticeable slump to his shoulders as he turned away.

Kilarny called the three witnesses, one at a time, and each of them repeated the story exactly as Rowry had told it. Kilarny couldn't keep the ghost of a grin from his mouth as he dismissed the last of the three witnesses. "I believe that's all, Your Honor. We have no further defense."

"Any further witnesses?" Chambers asked.

"This investigation broke so quickly that I didn't have time to gather all my witnesses," Kearns protested. "I can get half of the town to tell what a likable man Chubby Inman was to be cut down—"

"I know," Chambers said wearily. "We're not thinking about the same man, Mr. Kearns. You're painting a picture of a worthy citizen. I've heard about a dangerous, half-crazed man, armed and full of hate. If you haven't anything else to say, will you please sit down."

Kearns slunk to his chair.

"Mayor Reaves, would you like to say something?"

Reaves stood. He looked slowly about the room, and Rowry knew he was going to make a speech. Reaves rarely lost an opportunity to make a few political points.

"I deplore this unfortunate happening," he started out. "I, too, knew Chubby. He was the most likable of men, a happy man—"

"Except when he was drinking," Chambers said dryly.

Reaves looked pained. "I was going to say that, Your Honor. I wish I could change what happened, but I cannot. I do not want my law officers going around shooting citizens indiscriminately. But in this case, I guess it was necessary."

"I'd say it was," Chambers snapped. "It was a killing in the line of self-defense, clearly provoked by the victim. I declare that there is no blame or guilt to be placed on Deputy Saxton. He performed his duty admirably. I declare this hearing is over."

Rowry took the first relieved breath he had taken since entering the room. Kilarny came over to him and wrung his hand.

"I can't thank you enough," Rowry said.

Kilarny made a deprecatory slash with his hand. "For what? Next time, give me something tough."

"This was tough enough for me," Rowry said.

Butler came over and clapped him on the back. "What did I tell you? I told you how it'd be."

"I couldn't help doing a little worrying," Rowry confessed.

Butler grinned. "You know something? I did some of that, too. I didn't want to lose my deputy."

Rowry looked across the room, and Kearns was staring at him with malignant eyes. "Kearns isn't very happy about the outcome," he remarked.

Kilarny turned and looked in Kearns's direction. He laughed. "You know, I hope to see him looking unhappy a hundred times more."

"But not with me caught in the middle," Rowry said.

Kilarny chuckled. "No. I'd say you've had enough of a strain for a while."

"Not for a while," Rowry corrected. "For a lifetime."

CHAPTER 10

Ord upended the bottle and let the fiery liquid gush down his throat. Verl Wellman grabbed the bottle out of Ord's hand, spilling some of the liquid.

"Look what you did," Ord said indignantly. "You made me spill it. And that's the last bottle. We ain't got no more money to buy another one."

The four sat drinking in Morley's old, abandoned barn on the outskirts of town. For the past week, they hadn't dared go into town lest Butler and Rowry flash their teeth at them. Cleavers had bought the bottle for them and gotten it out of town. Cleavers was one of the town's ne'er-do-wells, and it had cost the four an extra dollar to get the bottle.

"It's all your fault," Dent Edison said accusingly. "It wouldn't have happened if you weren't making such a hog out of yourself."

Ord looked angrily at Edison. He had noticed something peculiar. The more their money shrank, the more quarrels they had. The last few days they had done nothing but snap at each other. Maybe if they were allowed to go into town like everybody else, things wouldn't be strained.

Wellman drank and handed the bottle to Chad Duncan. Precious little of the whiskey remained. "I heard that damned brother of yours beat the investigation," he said sullenly. "I was hoping he'd lose his job and be run out of town."

"You think I wasn't?" Ord asked heatedly. "Ever since we jumped him, he does nothing but stare at me."

"Does he know?" Duncan asked.

"He hasn't said so, but he knows," Ord replied bleakly. "I'm positive that's why Butler and him are on us so hard."

"Maybe we could try jumping him again," Edison suggested. "I enjoyed that evening. Maybe next time we can teach him a lesson he'll never forget."

"You're forgetting something," Ord sneered. "He shot Chubby Inman, even when Inman had a gun on him. Rowry's quick. I know. I've seen him practice. I've seen him shoot a quail, sitting on the ground, and it wasn't too close. It takes a real good shot to be able to do that. He won't be so easy to catch off guard next time."

"You sound like you're scared of him," Duncan sneered.

Ord's face flamed, but he gave Duncan's words some thought before he answered. "You're damn right I am," he said. "Tell me you're not scared to face him."

Duncan spat on the ground. "I wouldn't want that," he replied.

The silence fell heavy and grinding on the four. Only two had admitted it, but all four were fearful of Butler and Rowry.

"Looks like we'll spend the rest of our lives sneaking around and drinking in an old, abandoned barn," Wellman said.

Ord turned Wellman's words over in his mind. The longer he thought about them, the less he liked them. "You could be right, Verl, unless we get out of town."

"How in the hell are we going to do that?" Wellman demanded. "We haven't got enough money between us to buy another bottle."

An idea was beginning to form in Ord's head. He was silent a moment, letting it grow. "Maybe there's a way we could all get out of this miserable town. I don't think any of us is too crazy about it."

Three heads thought about it, then slowly began shaking. "I'd leave in a minute if I had the means," Wellman said. "There's no pleasure living here with your old man snapping at your heels all the time."

Ord had the same problem, only in his case it was a brother constantly nagging at him. Jesus Christ, he didn't have a peaceful moment with Rowry keeping an eye on every move he made. He knew that Dent and Chad had the same problems with their families. They had talked about it many times.

The idea clicked into place, and it had a brilliance that blinded him. He sat up straight and exclaimed, "I've got it."

"Be quiet," Wellman said sarcastically to the other two. "The genius is about to give us the master plan."

"It'd get all four of us out of this stinking town," Ord said, unperturbed. "We'd have money in our pockets."

"Didn't I tell you he was a genius?" Wellman asked.

Ord shrugged. "It's all right with me if you don't want to hear it." He stared obstinately at a wall of the barn.

Curiosity worked on Edison and Duncan, and Duncan said, "Will you shut up, Wellman, and let him talk. Maybe he has got an idea."

Wellman's laugh had a cutting edge. "Sure he has." He couldn't stop snickering. "It'll put money in our pockets. Anybody who believes that is ready for the crazy house."

Ord remained silent. If he knew these three, and he did, they would be demanding to know what he had in mind.

Wellman broke the long silence. "Come on, Ord. Tell us what the master's got in his head."

"I know of a place where we could get all the money we need," Ord said slowly.

Wellman cackled. "Sure you do. All we have to do is to ask for it."

Ord shook his head. "Just about the same thing. Taking it will be easy."

He had their full attention, and they stared at him with burning eyes. Tantalizingly, he remained silent again.

"Come on," Wellman said impatiently. "Are you going to tell us or not?"

"It's been right under our noses all the time," Ord said and grinned. "All we have to do is to take it."

He had piqued their curiosity now; they got to their feet and stood in a ring about him. "Are you going to tell us or not?" Wellman demanded.

Ord laughed shortly. "At the bank," he said.

Wellman turned angry. "You think that's funny, stringing us along like this. Why, goddamn it—" He raised a threatening hand.

"Don't try it," Ord snapped. "I'm not stringing you along."

"Sure you ain't," Wellman said. "All I have to do is to go up to my Pa and say, 'Please, Pa, we need some money,' and he'll hand it over to me."

"We don't have to ask nobody," Ord said, unruffled. "We'll just walk in and take it."

Wellman shook his head. "Now I *know* you're crazy."

"You can get the key to the front door, can't you?" Ord asked. "Your old man probably keeps the combination to the vault somewhere in the house. He has to in case he loses or forgets the combination." He heard the sharp inhalation of breath. The plan was so daring that it dazzled them.

"My God," Duncan said unbelievingly. "He *is* a genius."

Edison bobbed his head, grinning broadly.

"I don't know," Wellman said dubiously. "If Pa caught me at it, he'd knock the hell out of me."

"Then just don't let him catch you," Ord said and chuckled. All of them were tempted by the plan, but Ord thought he detected an unknown fear in them holding them back. "Oh hell," he said. "If you're too scared to try something, then stay in this town and rot."

Wellman was breathing faster, and his eyes were beginning to shine. "Suppose I did get my hands on the key and found the combination. When do you think we should try it?"

"Why not tonight?" Ord proposed. "It looks like rain coming up. We couldn't pick a better night."

Duncan and Edison were swept away by the confidence in Ord's words. "Come on, Verl. We're depending on you."

Wellman still held back. "I don't know," he said doubtfully.

"Are you afraid of trying something as big as this?" Ord taunted him. "We've all got horses. We'll lock the door behind us as we leave. They'll never be able to figure out what happened."

"You're right," Wellman exclaimed. "After tonight, there'll be no more of Pa's abuse."

Ord nodded. "I thought you'd see it that way. There's an alley running by the bank. We'll meet there at ten o'clock. Verl, if you can't get your hands on the combination, we'll simply put it off until another night."

Now Wellman was picked up and carried by Ord's confidence. "I'll get it," he said buoyantly. "I'll see you all at ten o'clock."

"Better wear a slicker," Ord advised. "And pray that we need those slickers." He grinned at all of them. He was swelling with pride. He was a big and important man. Hadn't he proven it by the way the others listened to him?

CHAPTER 11

Butler didn't get in until a little after eleven. "I attended Inman's funeral," he said in explanation of his unusual tardiness.

Rowry nodded bleakly. "I thought that was where you were." He tried to say it casually, but just the thought of Inman being buried put a tightness in his throat. "Big crowd?"

"Surprisingly so," Butler replied. "Chubby had a lot of friends in this town."

That was so, Rowry thought gravely. And those friends would resent the shooting for a long time. He was just as well off not going to that funeral.

Butler shuffled through some papers, but his mind wasn't on getting back to work. "Abby was there," he suddenly announced.

Rowry nodded. "I saw her last night. She said she might go." His eyes were withdrawn as he went over their talk.

"What did she have to say?" Butler asked.

"About what?"

Butler snorted. Rowry knew what he was talking about. "About the whole mess," he replied. "The shooting and the investigation." He was pretty sure what Abby and Rowry had talked about. These were the biggest events that had happened in this town for a long while.

"Abby said I had to quit thinking about it. The shooting wasn't my fault. If I didn't quite thinking about it, I'd drive myself crazy."

"She's right," Butler said. "That's one smart woman. Are you going to let her get away from you?"

"I hope I'm not," Rowry replied and smiled. He was silent for a long while, then said, "Creed, how does one go about getting something off his mind? Everybody I see looking at me looks like they've got a weighing in their eyes."

"It's only as heavy as you let it be," Butler said matter-of-factly. "Time's the greatest healer. A few days, a few weeks, and people will have forgotten it. But you've got to be patient. You can't force it."

"That's hard to do," Rowry said.

Butler shook his head. He understood exactly how Rowry felt, but that was the viewpoint of youth. It took age for a man to learn to be patient. "It'll pass, Rowry."

Rowry gave him a slight, negative shake of his head. The gesture said, "I don't believe you."

It would pass. Butler knew that, but the big trouble was getting Rowry to believe it. "Want me to take the rounds today?" he asked.

Rowry measured him with a long stare. "Say what you mean, Creed," he snapped.

Butler sighed. Rowry was as touchy as a cat with a mashed He knew what Butler meant. Butler was trying to save him fro meeting people and having to speak to them. Rowry resented tha.

"You're going ahead anyway," Butler growled. "Nothing I can say will stop you. But let me tell you something. Regardless of what you think you see in people's eyes, ignore it. Pass them right on by. This will pass."

Rowry grinned twistedly. He picked up his rifle. "The passing is what is killing me. I'm all right, Creed."

"Good man," Butler said heartily. "Hadn't you better take your slicker? A few drops were coming down when I came in."

Rowry glanced out of the window. "Maybe I'd better wear it. It's sure getting black out there." He didn't like wearing a slicker. They built up a heat in a man until he sweat enough to make him as dripping wet as the actual rainfall. Rainfall and a slicker made a proposition where a man couldn't win.

He struggled into his slicker. "Damned things," he grumbled. "Make a man sweat like a hog."

Butler agreed. "But without one, you're soaked to the skin."

"Yep," Rowry said sourly. He stepped outside. He hadn't gone a block before the rain started in earnest. Rowry had seen harder rains, but this one would do. The farmers would welcome it; the city people would complain bitterly about the inconvenience.

He passed few people on the street, and he appreciated that the rain eliminated that dreaded weighing of eyes. Most people would be gathered in the saloons or in the stores. Rowry didn't have to enter any of those.

He finished his round and returned to the office. He stripped off the slicker and dropped it in a corner of the room. He found a piece of cloth and dried off his rifle. "Coming down pretty good," he remarked.

Butler nodded. "Any trouble?"

"None. Few people out in this."

"The next round will be that much easier," Butler said seriously. "It's like whittling on a stick. Every shaving makes the stick that much smaller. Believe me, Rowry, I know. I know what you're going through. I've been through all this."

wry considered his words, then nodded. Butler was an old d, with plenty of experience behind his words. His advice had ver steered Rowry wrong before.

A couple of hours passed, and Rowry stood. "Let me take it, Creed."

"Sure you want to?" Butler asked gruffly. Wet weather always brought out the little devils of pain in his legs, and he would gladly accept Rowry's offer. Still, he didn't want to push off anything onto him.

"I want to," Rowry said briefly. "I figure I got so many rounds to make before people accept it as just being a normal thing." He grinned at Butler. "You said something about with each shaving, the stick is smaller."

"Exactly, Rowry." Butler put his bootheels up on the desk and was slouched in his chair as he watched Rowry go out. He mustn't get in the habit of dumping all the work on Rowry. It would be a simple thing to do. He had the age and authority on Rowry, and Rowry was always willing to take the rounds. No, he mustn't get in the habit—Butler's eyes were closed before he completed the thought.

Rowry's entrance awakened him. Butler yawned. "Still raining?"

"It's slowed down some," Rowry replied. He took off the slicker and dumped it in the corner. "Feet wet," he complained. "Damned rain runs off my slicker and into my boots."

Butler watched him sympathetically. Rowry wasn't a complainer. Butler knew what he was doing. The complaining kept Rowry from thinking about the heavier burden on his mind. "Run across anybody?" he asked casually.

"A few," Rowry said. "They were hurrying to get out of the rain. People won't venture out into this. It'll be a quiet day and night."

"Won't that be good, Rowry?"

Rowry nodded. "It'll be good."

Butler watched him through half-closed eyes. Rowry had whittled another shaving off the stick, but the stick still had some heft to it. But Butler thought the strain was beginning to slip off Rowry's face. Closing his mind to everything but work was doing the trick, he thought with pleasure.

Rowry made another round before supper. When he returned, Butler insisted they eat supper together at Ma Atkins'. His presence might keep some lamebrain from making a brash remark to Rowry. They weren't bothered during their meal. They sat alone at a table at the far side of the room. Heads craned, then bent closer together, and Butler knew the conversations had to be about Rowry. A couple of times people seemed on the verge of coming over to their table, then reconsidered and went on out of the restaurant. It was just as well they did.

They finished the meal and went out into the rainy night. It was usually light at this hour, but the lowering clouds had cut off every vestige of light. It was going to be a dark and gloomy night. But maybe that was all to the good. The inclement weather would keep people home.

"I know what you mean," Butler grumbled on the way back to the office. "These damned slickers aren't made the right length. They hit you at the knees, and the water runs down onto your pants leg until it's soaked. Then it trickles down into your boots. Damn, this moisture is killing my legs. Let me give you a piece of advice, Rowry. Don't ever get old. That's when all the hidden infirmities jump out on you."

Rowry grinned. "You got a way of forestalling that old age?"

"Not yet, but I'm going to work on it."

"If you find it, it'll make you a rich man," Rowry said and laughed.

Butler was still grumbling when they reached the office, and Rowry said, "Creed, I know it's supposed to be your night on. But why don't you go on home and rest those aching legs. You know it's going to be a quiet night with this kind of weather. I can handle it—unless you're beginning to doubt that."

"You know better than that, Rowry," Butler said severely. He had a room in the hotel, and the thought of tucking into that room, particularly on such a rainy night, had its appeal. He could stretch out and rest those aching legs. "Sure you want to do it?"

"I asked for it, didn't I?"

Butler sighed with pleasure. He knew he was giving in to a weakness, but he couldn't resist the temptation. He turned to go out the

door and paused there a moment. "Make the round about ten
o'clock tonight. One will be enough tonight. People won't be out,
and what few are won't have any mischief on their minds."

"All right, if you think so, Creed."

"I think so," Butler said crisply. He stepped outside and quickened his stride to get out of this rain and back to that room.

Rowry put his heels up. He was too long to really find a comfortable position. He kept squirming until he found the best one he
could. Even slouching down in the chair, he couldn't get the back of
the chair out of his neck. He listened to the patter of raindrops on
the window, stronger when a sharp gust of wind seized them and
flung them at the glass. A rotten night, he thought. He was just as
happy he didn't have to plod about in it for too long. Maybe he
could doze a little before he started out on the ten o'clock round.

He came to with a start. Damned if he hadn't done more than just
doze off; he had slept soundly. He glanced at the clock, and it was
twenty minutes until ten o'clock. He had time to stretch the kinks out
of his neck before he went out. He was damned glad this wasn't a
winter night. It would be pure hell with all this moisture and the
wind behind it. He'd be plowing through deep snow.

He kept turning his head, trying to work that kink out of his neck.
Sleeping in that awkward position had readily put a bend in it. For a
few seconds, he thought it might be permanent.

He got the kink out and massaged his neck for a few moments.
"That's better," he grunted. He glanced at the clock again. The long
hand had crept up to twelve minutes of ten. He could go now. It
might be a little early, but he couldn't see any harm in that.

He buttoned his slicker up to his neck. The damned thing felt
damp from his previous excursions. He thought a moment, then par-
tially unbuttoned the slicker and tucked his rifle inside the protective
cover. There was no sense getting the rifle wet, then having to dry
and oil it. He wouldn't need it on such a night.

He rebuttoned the slicker and stepped outside, the rifle clamped
under his right arm. It was an awkward way to carry it, and he
scowled as the wind quickened, dashing a stinging spray of rain into
his face. One hell of a night, he thought morosely.

It was raining harder than it had been earlier, and the clouds were so low Rowry could almost swear he could reach up and touch them. Visibility was poor, and he had to keep a sharp eye out for puddles. His boots were wet enough as they were.

He looked wistfully at each building or house that had a light. The rain and fog put an inviting patina on each shine of light, and it all looked so inviting. The faster he finished this round, the quicker he could get back to shelter.

He noticed one thing that momentarily struck him as odd. Usually, on a round, he would see a dozen or more dogs and cats, all busy with their night or day prowling. Tonight, he didn't see a single animal. He guessed animals were smarter than to be out on a night like this. Only a human was that stupid.

Rowry was glad he had relieved Creed before he finished half of his tour. His boots were thoroughly soaked, and it would be even worse before he finished. The wind prevented him from hearing the squishing of his feet inside his boots, but he knew they were. They couldn't be otherwise.

He came out onto Main Street after he finished covering the residential district. This was wasted effort, he thought sourly. Nobody would be out in weather like this. This was a rotten job in such weather. He grinned wryly. Maybe that hearing had soured his outlook. Ordinarily, he was completely satisfied with what he was doing.

He started out at the end of Main Street and slowly made his way down it, stopping momentarily to check the doors of every building that had no light in it. He would have to cover the other side of the street when he was through with this side. He paused briefly to rattle the doorknobs, and all of them were secure. He was almost opposite the Wellman Bank when a flash of color caught his attention. For a moment, he wasn't sure of what he saw. Visibility was poor. He stared hard, trying to get a better view. He nodded grimly. Yes, that quick flash wasn't a mirage. There were four indistinct figures moving toward the mouth of the alley that ran beside the bank. Even as he hesitated, the four slipped around the corner and vanished.

Rowry wrestled with a problem. Should he dash into that alley and see what those four had been up to? Their appearance so near the bank was suspicious in itself, and ducking into the alley only made it more so. No, he decided. He would be a damned fool to run into that alley. His mind picked at the problem. If they had been up to something illegal, they probably had horses tethered in that alley. He could wait until they came riding out, then order them to halt. He nodded as he arrived at his decision, unbuttoned his slicker, and took the rifle from under its cover. There would be four against him. He patted the rifle butt. It would cut down the odds, particularly on a night like this.

His eyes were straining to pick them out the moment they reappeared; his ears were tuned to hear any sound that would announce their coming.

He heard the sloshy sound of a hoof being planted on a wet surface, and the first one appeared, riding out of the alley. Rowry let out a small sigh of relief. His guess had been right on the nose. It could have turned out differently. They could have ridden through the alley and come out at the other end. He would wait until all four were in sight.

He lifted the rifle butt and planted it against his shoulder. The second rider appeared, followed in rapid succession by the other two.

"Halt," Rowry bellowed. "This is the law."

Did he hear a grunt of surprise, or was he only imagining things? They reacted more quickly than he had expected. All four spun their horses and took off down the street in the opposite direction. They were bent low over their mounts' necks, and Rowry gritted his teeth. He shouldn't have given them that warning, but his doubts about shooting had vanished. They had been up to something illegal, or they wouldn't be riding so hard, trying to get away from here.

Rowry fired two shots in quick succession, and he didn't see a single rider waver or slump from his saddle. Rowry had always prided himself on his marksmanship, and he cursed at his lack of results, even though he had been shooting at moving targets on a misty night. The four riders were strung out now in single file, and Rowry knew his chances of bagging them were growing slimmer with each passing second. He dropped to one knee to steady his shooting and aimed at the last rider in the line. He pulled the trigger and felt the familiar thump as the butt slammed into his shoulder. He thought the rider reared up, but for a moment, he couldn't be sure he had scored. Then the rider threw up his arms and fell out of the saddle. He landed heavily, and the riderless horse galloped on after the other riders.

Well, he had gotten one of them, Rowry thought. His shooting hadn't been completely futile.

He stood and advanced toward the spot where he had seen the rider fall. The man, too, wore a yellow slicker, and the splash of color stood out.

Rowry reached the body. It was sprawled face down on the street; only a short while ago Rowry had looked at this same flaccid form of death. That peculiar sickness came back to his stomach, then he clamped a hard mental hand on his unease, chasing it away.

He still couldn't see who the rider was, and Rowry toed the body over on its back. He couldn't plainly make out the face, but he knew, for his stomach knotted, and the sour taste of bile filled his mouth. "God Almighty," he said hoarsely. "It's Ord."

Rowry had no idea how much time passed, for there was no measuring time at a moment like this. He bent closer to the body. Maybe he had been mistaken. His hope was futile. It was the face he knew so well.

"Ord, you've been headed for something like this for a long time," he muttered. He felt no sorrow, no regret. Any closeness between them had vanished a long time ago. Then he thought of Sid, and the regret came in wave after wave. Sid would never forgive him.

He wished he could just turn and walk away, but he couldn't leave Ord's body in the rain. He stood there with his head hanging low, and his stomach rose and heaved a couple of times. Rowry made a supreme effort and got his sickness under control.

He heard voices in the distance, and they were loud and excited enough that he could make out the words.

"Jed," a voice called. "Where do you think that shooting was?"

"I think it was farther down the street," another voice replied.

"Down here." Rowry raised his voice to its limit. One thing would be taken off him. He wouldn't have to stand here beside the body with its accusing eyes.

Six men came out of the rainy, foggy night, and one of them spotted Rowry and recognized him. "Was that you, Deputy, doing all that shooting?"

"Yes," Rowry replied simply. "Four men tried to rob the bank tonight. I just happened to be passing by. I managed to stop one of them. The others got away." He stepped aside so that the men could get a better view of the body lying on the ground.

One of them bent low over Ord, and he seemed to remain in that position for an eternity. Then he straightened, and his voice had a queer strain. "Jesus Christ, it's Ord. You shot your own brother."

"He was one of the robbers," Rowry said, no emotion in his voice. "I want you men to take him to the undertaker. I've got to report this to Creed as fast as I can."

He couldn't tell what those staring faces meant. He read fear, distrust and uneasiness. He couldn't blame a one of them. It wasn't often that a man killed his own brother.

CHAPTER 12

Rowry walked into the hotel where Creed lived. He was shaking all over. His knees threatened to buckle on him, dumping him on the floor.

He made it up to the desk, and old Priam Quincy, the night clerk, dozed behind it. Quincy was old in his thoughts and his motions, and night clerking was the only job he could even begin to handle.

Rowry shouted at him a half-dozen times before he got through the sleepy fog that surrounded Quincy. Damn this old man's deafness. Rowry was ready to go around the counter and shake him awake when Quincy opened his eyes.

He stared blankly at Rowry, and slow recognition filtered into his eyes. "No reason to do all that shouting," he said indignantly. "I heard you the first time you called my name."

Rowry understood the testiness in the old man's voice. Priam was trying to deny that he was hard of hearing and sleeping on the job. "I've got to see Creed. Right now," Rowry snapped.

Priam looked doubtfully at him. "I imagine Creed's sleeping by now. He won't look with favor at being woke up."

"Goddamn it," Rowry almost shouted. "This is important."

Priam still had that dubious look on his face. "I don't know. I've seen Creed woke up once or twice before. He was powerful mad."

Rowry could no longer stand bandying words with the old man. He reached over the counter with his free hand, grabbed Priam by the shoulder, and said frantically, "I told you this is important."

Priam jerked away, and a touch of fear was in his eyes. "You go up and wake him up," he said in a trembling voice. "I ain't going to be responsible. He's in room three twelve."

"I know his room," Rowry snapped. It would have been better if he had gone straight to Creed's room without wasting all that time talking to Quincy, but he had thought it best that he notify the old man of his presence in the hotel.

He climbed the steps, forcing his shaking legs to carry him another step higher. He turned off on the third floor and moved down the dimly lighted hall, stopping before the door of 312. He sucked in a deep breath to fortify himself, then rapped on the door. He didn't wait long before he knocked again. Creed was always a hard sleeper.

He beat on the door with his clenched fist and yelled, "Creed, goddamn it, open this door."

He heard an unhappy voice mutter, "Who's there? What do you want?"

"It's Rowry, Creed. I've got to talk to you." He heard Creed's soft swearing and the patter of bare feet.

Butler opened the door, and his expression was grim. He was barefoot and wore his light summer underwear. "Rowry," he started heatedly. "You better have something to tell me. First night I'd gotten into a good night's sleep in a long time. Damn—"

Rowry waved him quiet and brushed by him. He walked into the room and sat down before his legs carried out their threat and dumped him. "Some trouble at the bank, Creed, just a little while ago. I happened to be coming by it when I caught a glimpse of four men. They had just come out of the bank and ducked into the alley before I could get to them." He paused. That damned shaking was intensifying.

Butler was wide awake now, and his eyes were narrowed as he listened. "Go on," he said impatiently.

"I decided not to try and chase them into the alley," Rowry continued. "I waited until they came back out. I figured they had horses in that alley."

"That was smart," Butler approved. "They did come out?"

Rowry nodded. "They could've gone on down the alley to the other end." His tone was wry.

"But they didn't. A man can drive himself crazy if he tries to consider all the possibilities that could happen."

"They came out," Rowry said dully. "All of them mounted. I waited until all four were in sight. I called to them to halt, and they just dug in their heels. I got off two shots and missed both." Again he was silent, reliving that dreadful moment.

"Will you get on with it?" Butler yelled.

"They fell into a single file, driving as hard as they could. I dropped to one knee to get a steady shot. They were getting close to a corner, and if they turned it, they were gone. I took all the time I dared in aiming. I only got a clear sight at the last rider. I shot, and he fell." He was breathing in hard, racking breaths. "I walked up to him and toed him over—" He gulped, unable to say anything more at the moment.

"For God's sake," Butler begged. "Did you know him?"

"I knew him all right," Rowry whispered. "It was Ord. I killed him."

"Jesus Christ!" Butler's words came out shrilly, sounding almost like a whistle. "You're sure? Forget that, Rowry. That was a stupid question."

"It was him all right," Rowry said. "His horse galloped along with the others. They went around that corner before I could get another shot at them. You can figure out who they were."

Butler nodded, his craggy face set in tough lines. "Wellman, Duncan and Edison. Those four were always together. But how do you know they robbed the bank?"

"It has to figure," Rowry replied. "They had to be coming out of the bank. And their horses were in that alley. Everything ties up."

"I guess it does," Butler muttered. "Anything more?"

"I couldn't leave Ord lying out in the rain, could I?"

Butler shook his head. "You couldn't."

"I stayed there until some men came up, calling to each other. They'd heard the shooting, but they didn't know where it was. I called them over and stepped aside so they could get a good look at what was on the ground."

"Who were they?" Butler asked practically.

Rowry shook his head. "With the rain and all, I didn't get a good look at them. I guess I was too rattled to even ask their names."

Butler nodded again. "Understandable. Did you say anything to them?"

Rowry bobbed his head. God, he was weary. Just telling Butler about this was sucking all the strength out of him. "I told them there'd been a bank robbery, that I'd got one of them. One of them bent over Ord, and when he straightened, there was a queer look on his face."

"I can imagine," Butler said dryly. "He recognized Ord?"

"He did. I asked them to see that Ord got to the undertaker. I told them I had to report to you as quick as I could."

"You did exactly right," Butler said crisply. He stood, put on his pants, then sat down on the edge of the bed to tug on his boots. "I'll go down to the undertaker's first, then I'll go to the office. When this gets out, I expect there'll be a lot of traffic there. Rowry, go on home. You've had enough tonight."

Rowry started to shake his head, and Butler roared. "Tonight I'm not arguing with you. I mean what I said."

Rowry gave in. "Creed, before I go home, I have to tell Abby about this. I don't want her hearing this from somebody else."

"I can understand that. Get on over there, then get home. Now what's that miserable look on your face for?"

"I've got to tell Sid," Rowry said slowly. "It'll be the hardest thing I've ever had to do."

There was pure pity on Butler's face. "Wish there was something I could do to help, but this time you'll have to handle it alone."

"Sure," Rowry said. He stood, and the trembling had gone out of his legs. He was grateful for that. In the shape they'd been in when he came here, they wouldn't have carried him a block. He paused at the door. "Thanks for everything, Creed."

"For what?" Butler snorted. "You only did what you had to do. I wouldn't have you on the payroll if you hadn't. One other thing, Rowry. Stop in Kilarny's office first thing in the morning."

"What for?" Rowry asked.

"I want Kilarny to know everything that happened tonight. I've got a hunch the lid's going to blow off of hell when this gets out. Kilarny's a good man to have with you."

"I'll see him, Creed," Rowry said and went out of the door. He closed the door behind him, then leaned against it a moment, his brow furrowed. Did Butler have some hidden meaning behind his words about Kilarny? The long, tearing sigh sounded as though it came from the pit of his stomach.

CHAPTER 13

It was still raining when Rowry left the hotel, and he buttoned the slicker up to his throat. This was a buster of a storm, and it could last three or four days. He put the rifle back under his slicker, although he had gotten it thoroughly wet. He would have to dry and oil it when he got home.

A light was on in the Barnett home when he reached it. Rowry was relieved. If Abby wasn't still up, some of the Barnett family were.

He knocked firmly on the door. He hoped it would be answered by Abby; he didn't relish the thought of telling his story to the other members of the family.

The door opened, and it was Bill Barnett, Abby's father. Rowry didn't let his disappointment show. He liked the man, and he thought Bill returned the feeling.

"Hello, Bill," he said, trying to put warmth into his voice. "Is Abby in?"

"Come in, come in," Barnett said. "Do you have to paddle around on this kind of night?" He chuckled at his weak witticism.

"On duty," Rowry replied. "I shouldn't come in. I'll drip all over your floor."

"You could leave your slicker on the porch, couldn't you? I'll just warm up the coffee. Won't take a minute. I'll bet a cup of hot coffee would go down good."

"I really haven't got time for it," Rowry said. "Could I just talk to Abby? It's important."

Barnett gave him an odd glance. "She's gone to bed. I was just doing a little reading before I turned in."

"I wouldn't want you to wake her," Rowry said. Perhaps his disappointment came through in his face or his voice. Whichever it was, Barnett caught it.

"You said it was important, didn't you?" At Rowry's nod, he asked, "Did something bad happen tonight?"

Rowry felt his throat tighten. News ran quickly through a small town. Perhaps Barnett had already heard something about the shooting. "No," he said, trying to keep his voice steady. "I just wanted to talk to Abby."

Barnett gave him a slow appraisal, then said, "She went to her room not fifteen minutes ago. I remember when I was courting how important a talk could be. I'll see if she's awake."

Barnett had jumped to the wrong conclusion, and Rowry was glad. "If she isn't awake, don't rouse her," he said.

Barnett nodded and left the room. Five minutes passed before Abby came in. A gray wrapper was buttoned to the throat, and she had a towel wrapped turbanlike on her head.

"You would pick tonight to come by," she said in wry resignation. "I just washed my hair."

"I'm sorry, Abby, but I had to tell you this before someone else did."

She caught the gravity in his tone, and alarm filled her eyes. "Did something bad happen tonight, Rowry?"

It was the same question her father had asked, and Rowry grimaced. "There was a bank robbery, Abby," he said in a low voice. "Four men. I was across the street and with the rain and all, I couldn't see them too plainly. They had horses in an alley, and I waited for them to come out. I yelled halt, but they didn't stop. I fired two shots at them, but it wasn't a good night for shooting. I settled down and fired the last time. One of them tumbled out of his saddle."

The strain had grown more apparent in his voice, and Abby asked sharply, "You knew him, didn't you?"

The trembling was starting in Rowry's hands again. "Not then. Not until I walked up and turned him over." His mouth was so dry he didn't know if he could get the name out. He tried, and it came out a squeak. "It was Ord."

She stared at him with horror-filled eyes. "Oh no, Rowry."

"Yes," he said and dared to meet her eyes. "I didn't know when I fired. It was the same four who jumped me before. I know it was. The other three got away."

She came up to him and put her arms around him. He smelled her fresh sweetness. "You had to do it, Rowry," she said consolingly. "It was your job."

He groaned deep in his throat. Butler had said practically the same thing. No matter how many people said it, it couldn't remove the throbbing blow of the incident.

"Come over here and sit down," she said.

He sank gratefully onto the sofa, and Abby said, "You're shaking. I'm going to get some coffee."

He had refused her father on the same offer, but now the prospect seemed more enticing. "I'd like that," he said simply.

She came back in a few minutes with the coffeepot and two cups. She filled his cup and handed it to him. "I put a little whiskey in that cup," she said. "You need it. You're wet and cold."

He nodded gratefully and gulped down big mouthfuls of the stout brew. She hadn't put a little whiskey in the cup. She had laced the coffee good. He could feel the warmth begin to steal through him. "Thank you, Abby," he said.

"You look better," she said, looking critically at him. "You've got more color in your face."

He grimaced. "Must be a weakness in me. I was damned near the breaking point when I came here."

"It wasn't a weakness," she said sharply. "You had every right to that feeling."

She offered to refill his cup, and Rowry shook his head. "This will do, Abby. I had to tell you before some loose tongue rushes here to dump this news on you."

"I'm glad you did," she said sincerely. "It gives me time to be ready to face it when it breaks out."

He nodded. That was exactly what he had in mind. How he appreciated this woman. There was no withdrawal in her—perhaps a little shock at first hearing the news, but that was quickly gone. "This gives me enough courage to go and face Sid," he said hollowly.

She sucked in her breath. "I'd forgotten. This is going to be hard on him."

"It'll come down on him like a mountain," he said simply. He shook his head. "I really don't know how he'll react." He stared blankly at nothing for a long moment, then said, "Well, it has to be done."

She walked to the door with him and came into his arms for a brief moment. "My clothes are damp," he warned her. "That slicker sweat all over me."

That only put more fervor into her embrace. "Things will turn out all right, Rowry," she said and kissed him.

"I hope you're right, Abby."

"I usually am," she retorted and followed it with a shaky laugh. He kissed her again and stepped out onto the porch. She stood in the doorway and watched while he slipped into his damp slicker. He raised a hand to her, and she said, "It'll turn out all right." Tears sounded very near the surface of her voice.

He walked back to the street without looking back. There was one hell of a woman. She understood a situation and said the right things to cover it.

The hollow in his stomach grew bigger and bigger with each step toward his house. What was he going to say to Sid? What was the best way to break it to him? Lord, he thought in despair. I don't know.

A light was on in the house. Sid was still up. Would that make it easier to tell him, or would it have been easier to awaken him, then tell him? Again Rowry didn't know.

He took off his slicker, and hung it and his sodden hat on their pegs in the kitchen.

Sid looked up from his chair. "I'll bet you're glad this night is over."

Sid was wrong there. Rowry would be gladder if this night had never started.

"Ord's not in," Sid said fretfully. "I thought he'd be in on a night like this."

Rowry felt his heart lurch, then lodge in his throat. Ord would never be in again. "We had a little trouble tonight," he said slowly.

Sid peered at him with interest. Rowry's reports of what had happened in town were among the few bright spots in his life. "What was it?" he asked eagerly.

"Attempted bank robbery," Rowry said thickly. "I came by just in time to take three shots at the robbers."

"Good for you," Sid said in glee. "Did you get any of them?"

Rowry fought against the choking in his throat. "I killed one of them," he said, his voice unnatural.

"Served him right," Sid said. "I'm proud of you, boy."

He couldn't look at his father as he said, "Pa, it was Ord."

He dared to look at his father, and Sid's eyes were wide with shock. "Ord? You killed Ord?"

"I didn't know who it was, Pa," Rowry said pleadingly. "Vision was poor. All I saw was a man in a slicker trying to get away. I cut down on him. When I walked up to him, I found out it was Ord. He was with the other three who got him into trouble before."

Sid's face was ghastly, and he shook all over. "You're saying you killed your brother? You're saying he was in on a bank robbery? That's a lie. Ord wouldn't do anything like that."

Rowry sighed. He'd expected this kind of reaction from Sid. "He did this time," he said flatly.

"I know why you killed him," Sid said shrilly. "You never liked Ord. I heard you quarreling with him too many times to remember." He fell silent, his face racked with agony. Then he began to cry, and it was the horrible kind. Tears rolled down his cheeks, and he made no sound. "I knew you hated him, but I didn't realize how much," he whispered.

Rowry didn't try to defend himself. As wrought up as Sid was, nothing he could say would do any good.

Sid cried for a good ten minutes, then got haltingly to his feet. He started for his room, and Rowry asked worriedly, "What are you going to do, Pa?"

"I'm getting out of this house," Sid snarled at him. "I'm going to my sister's. I wouldn't stay in this house another minute, not with a murderer."

"Pa, that's not fair," Rowry begged. "I only did what I had to do."

"You did what you wanted to do," Sid flung back at him.

Rowry sat there dumbly until Sid reappeared. He was carrying a small valise. "Pa," Rowry begged. "You can't go out on a night like this."

"It'd be a hell of a lot better than staying in this house with you," Sid said angrily.

He got his old raincoat off its peg, donned it, and went out the door, letting it slam behind him.

The silence in the house grew worse with each passing minute. Voices out of the past came mockingly to him. He heard Ord speaking, then Sid. Rowry shook himself to be rid of the illusion. He felt as though he had been trampled under the hooves of a runaway herd. Nothing he could do or say would change the past. He got up and moved like a sleepwalker toward his room. Maybe sleep would help him shut out the memories of this night.

CHAPTER 14

Rowry thought he'd be lucky to get a couple of hours of sleep that night. He paced around the room trying to wear himself out, and sleep still wouldn't come. Toward dawn, he fell into an exhausted slumber.

He rose later than usual. Damn, he thought after his eyes were wide open. He was supposed to talk to Jeff Kilarny first thing this morning.

He dressed and shaved, noticing how hollow his eyes were. He looked like he'd been out on a week's binge. Halfheartedly, he set about preparing breakfast. The silence in the house was deafening. He wondered how Sid was doing with Aunt Edith. Edith had a waspish tongue, and whenever she and Sid were together, they bickered until they came to a full-blown quarrel. Rowry wondered if Sid would be driven back here. No, he thought morosely. Sid would never return, not as long as he believed Rowry had deliberately killed Ord.

The farther he got into breakfast, the more the thought of food sickened him. He abruptly abandoned the meal, putting away the food that could be used later.

He walked into Kilarny's office, and Jeff didn't have his usual good-natured look. In fact, he looked grim.

Rowry thought he knew why. Kilarny resented his being late. "Jeff, I'm sorry," he said. "I overslept. I—"

Kilarny waved him quiet. "Skip that, Rowry. Let's get to more important things."

"Did Butler see you last night?"

"He did," Kilarny replied.

"Then you know all about it—" Rowry started.

"I want to hear it from you. Don't leave out a word."

Rowry went through last night's events. Every time Kilarny thought he was omitting a detail, he stopped him and made him go through it more carefully. "You think it was the four who jumped you before?"

Rowry was surprised that Kilarny knew about that. "How did you know? Did Creed tell you?"

"He told me," Kilarny said. His face was tough. "I told you I didn't want you leaving out any details. Why do you think it was the same four?"

"Because Ord was with them. When you found one of them, you found the other three. They were inseparable."

Kilarny nodded, his face thoughtful. "I believe you. Go on."

Rowry wondered how many times he would have to tell of that grisly night. His voice was a little resentful as he went on. "They were outside the bank when I first saw them. I suspected they'd been inside."

"Did you recognize them then?"

Rowry shook his head. "I wasn't close enough, and the night was bad. It was hard to see."

"Then you didn't know them?"

"I told you that." Rowry's voice rose.

"Why did you suspect they had been inside the bank? Did you see them go in or come out?"

Rowry bristled at Kilarny's attitude. "It was just a gut feeling. Those four being near a bank just seemed odd. The night was so bad that hardly anybody was out. Yet those four were near the bank. Why do you keep hammering at me?"

"Because I'm afraid you'll be facing a lot more than what I'm giving you. I'm afraid you'll have to face a trial."

"A trial? Why? I shot a bank robber."

"That hasn't been proven yet," Kilarny said flatly. "Damn it, can't you see? I'm trying to find the holes in your story if there are any."

"They disappeared into the alley before I could cross the street. I figured they had horses there. I thought about it, then decided it was best to wait for them to come out."

"What if they hadn't?"

Rowry shrugged. "They did."

"Go ahead," Kilarny ordered.

"That was further proof to me, them coming riding out of the alley. Isn't it suspicious to you?"

"Enough," Kilarny admitted. "But I won't be judging your actions. What happened next?"

"They came riding out of the alley, and I missed two shots at them."

"Wasn't that unusual? A horseman is a big target. Don't bristle at me. Your reputation as a marksman is well known."

Rowry simmered down. It was a reasonable question. "You know the night was bad, with all that rain and fog. All of them were mounted, and they were moving targets. I guess I was a little excited.

I'd never tried to break up a bank robbery before." He looked beseechingly at Kilarny, whose face didn't change.

"There's more?" Kilarny said quietly.

Rowry sighed. There was a hell of a lot more. "At the first shot, they put their horses in a dead run, falling into single file. A corner was just ahead of them. If they got around that, I'd lost them. I dropped to one knee to get a steadier shot. I fired, and the last rider fell from his saddle."

"You didn't know who it was then?"

"No," Rowry said dully. "The other three whipped around a corner and the riderless horse galloped after them. I walked over to where that yellow slicker lay. The man was face down." Here came the most difficult part to tell. "I turned him over." Rowry's face was strained, and his voice hoarsened. "It was Ord."

"That's when you got the idea who the other three were?"

Rowry nodded dumbly. Oh God, he was reliving that horrible moment again. For a moment, he couldn't talk.

"It didn't end there," Kilarny suggested.

"No, it didn't. I couldn't just go on and leave Ord in the rain. I stood there, not sure of just what to do. Then I heard voices calling to each other. They were asking about the shots. I called out, and six of them came up and asked if I knew about the shooting. I told them I'd tried to break up a bank robbery and I'd gotten one of the robbers. I stepped out of the way so they could see."

"Did you know those six men?"

"If I did, I was so rattled, I didn't recognize them. One of them bent over Ord, and when he straightened, he looked at me funny. He wanted to know if I knew who it was. I knew," Rowry's voice almost broke. "The man knew who it was. He said, 'It's Ord,' and I nodded. I guess they didn't expect that, for they pulled back some and talked it over. I asked them to take Ord to the undertaker, and they agreed. I hurried over to Creed's hotel and told him what had happened."

"How did he take it?"

"He swore some as though it hit him as a hard surprise, then he sounded normal. He told me he was going to talk to you and told me to see you in the morning."

"That's everything you did last night?"

Rowry scowled at him. My God, when Kilarny said he wanted to know everything, he meant everything. "I stopped by to tell Abby what happened. I didn't want somebody else telling her."

"How did she accept it?"

"She was shocked, but she couldn't see any other way I could have handled it. She's a wonderful woman. I might have gone to pieces if it hadn't been for her support."

"She is," Kilarny said heartily. "That's all?"

"Just about," Rowry replied. "I went on home and told Sid all about it."

"How did he take it?"

"Hard." Rowry briefly closed his eyes. He could still visualize the agony in Sid's face and voice. "It broke him up, and he cried. He said I was nothing but a murderer, that Ord was a good boy and he would never be involved in a bank robbery."

"But you knew better. You'd just seen him involved in one."

"Yes." The dullness had returned to Rowry's voice. "Sid wouldn't even listen to me. Ord was his favorite. Had been ever since our mother died. Ma always favored Ord. I guess Sid felt obliged to take over. He wound up by saying he wouldn't stay in the same house with me. He packed up a few things and left."

"Didn't that worry you?"

"Not too much," Rowry said in a lifeless voice. "He was going to his sister. She'd take him in." He didn't speak to Kilarny about his doubts about that pair getting along. That was none of Kilarny's business.

"You didn't agree with your father's opinion of Ord?"

"He was close to being worthless as he could be," Rowry said. For the first time, a note of passion filled his voice. "He wouldn't work, he wouldn't take any responsibilities."

"You and Ord quarrel about that often?"

"If we were together, a day couldn't pass without a fuss. His shiftless ways bothered Sid, too, but Sid couldn't stop them either."

"Did many people know how you felt about Ord?"

Rowry frowned. That was an odd question. "Quite a few, I suspect," he said sharply. "I never tried to hide it. I was ashamed of him. I didn't want people connecting me with Ord."

Kilarny drummed on his desk with his fingertips. Something was bothering him.

"I didn't leave out anything," Rowry said.

Kilarny gave him a fleeting grin. "I have no doubt of that, Rowry. I was thinking of what Kearns is going to do with this case if it's presented to him." He looked squarely at Rowry. "And believe me, it will be."

Rowry frowned again. "Why should he be drawn into this?"

"I think you'll be accused of murder," Kilarny said slowly. He raised a hand, stopping Rowry's outbreak. "I've got a strange feeling about this."

"My God," Rowry said, appalled. "I was only doing what I was supposed to do."

Kilarny nodded. "I know that, you know that. But is it enough to convince a whole lot of other people?"

Rowry sat there, his face stunned. "I can't believe it," he muttered.

Kilarny smiled sympathetically. "I know. There are some days when it doesn't seem worthwhile to get out of bed. Go on back to the office and tell Creed about our talk. Just wait until something happens. I'm sorry to say this, Rowry. I'm afraid that something will happen."

CHAPTER 15

Rowry was still dazed when he got back to the office. Kilarny's words kept running through his mind, and the more he thought about them, the more confused he was.

Butler looked up at his entrance. "Get everything straightened out?"

"Not according to Kilarny," Rowry exploded. "He listened to everything I said, and, believe me, I didn't leave out a thing."

"I believe you," Butler grunted.

"Do you know what he said when I finished?" Rowry burst out. "He said I could go on trial. For murder." He almost yelled the last two words.

Butler nodded, and his face was sober. "I was afraid of that. Jeff and I talked that over last night."

Rowry breathed deeply to get his emotions under control. "That's about as unfair as anything I ever heard of," he said.

"Come on now," Butler said in sudden anger. "You've lived long enough to know there's nothing fair about life."

Rowry shook his head stubbornly. "Because a man does what he's supposed to do, somebody tries to hit him with a ridiculous charge? Who would bring it?"

Butler looked pityingly at him. "Joe Kearns, for one. This is just the sort of case he likes to get his teeth into. He could gain some glory. Mayor Reaves, for another. He was pretty upset about the Inman thing."

"Jesus Christ," Rowry said, stunned. "I can't believe it."

"Here now," Butler said crisply, "nothing's happened yet. All of this is speculation as to what could happen. Kilarny could be wrong, you know."

Rowry studied the craggy face. "But you don't think so."

"I don't know what to think, Rowry," Butler confessed. "All we can do is wait and see what happens."

On the surface, those were harmless words. Then why did that little shiver run through Rowry?

Rowry remained in the office, since Butler refused to let him take any of the rounds. "Goddamn it, Creed," Rowry said hotly. "Are you trying to keep me out of sight?"

Butler smiled bleakly at him. "That thought occurred to me," he confessed. "I don't want you talking to anybody until we know which direction this is headed. You can bet the town is buzzing with this this morning."

"Thanks for the complete trust," Rowry said bitterly.

"Oh, for God's sake, Rowry. Start using your head. I'm only trying to protect you."

It seemed an eternity before Butler returned from his round. "Anything happen here?" he asked.

"Why do you ask that?" Rowry asked sullenly.

"I thought some of the curiosity seekers might come by to get a look at you. A dozen people stopped me and tried to talk about it. Damn it, Rowry, get that look off your face. It's natural that people are talking about what happened last night. It was an unusual occurrence."

Rowry managed a wan grin. He could see now what Butler was doing for him. "Thanks, Creed. I appreciate what you're doing."

"Maybe it'll just blow away, Rowry."

"But you don't believe it?" Rowry's anger was returning.

"I don't believe it," Butler said flatly.

A couple of hours passed, and Butler was just about ready to go out again. He was buckling on his gun belt when Mayor Reaves came in. The mayor's face was flushed, and he was breathing hard. He acted as if Rowry weren't in the room as he said, "Marshal, I want you to arrest your deputy. Here are the formal charges, drawn up by Judge Chambers."

"Thinking as usual, aren't you, Mayor?" Butler said sarcastically. "What are the charges?"

The color burned brighter in Reaves's face. "I'm only doing what the people expect me to do," he said stiffly. "When a city employee uses his badge to settle a personal grudge against another, then I think it's time to remove that man from office."

Butler threw Rowry an imperative glance, stilling his outburst of indignation. "So you started all this, Mayor?" he asked bitingly. "When is this so-called trial supposed to start?"

"Tomorrow morning at nine o'clock," Reaves replied. "I suggest you lock up the culprit until the trial begins."

Again Butler's chilling eyes quieted Rowry. "What are you fearful of, Mayor? That Rowry will try to run?"

The stiffness remained in Reaves's tone. "I'm only saying he should be handled the same way as any other criminal."

Butler had taken all he could stand. His purpling face showed that. "Will you get out of here?" he roared. "Before I throw you out. If you're not satisfied with the way I run this office, then do something about it."

The rage in his face was overwhelming, and Reaves paled before it. "I'm not trying to tell you how to run this office—" he began.

"Get out of here," Butler roared. "I won't tell you again."

Reaves backed to the door and tried to stand his ground there. "We expect you to bring Rowry to the trial at nine."

Butler took a couple of steps toward him, and his anger was awesome. Reaves turned and fled.

When Butler retook his chair, he was too angry to speak. Rowry watched him regain his composure and said, "You better lock me up, Creed."

Butler stared at him in utter disbelief. "What the hell's gotten into you?"

"I don't want you to get in any trouble because of me," Rowry replied.

"You know me better than that," Butler said. "Now tell me what's really on your mind."

Rowry grinned painfully. He had never been able to hide much from Butler. "I need a place to sleep, Creed. I don't want to go back to the house. The damned silence in it yells at me."

"At least that's honest," Butler snorted. "It might be the smartest thing to do. I don't want you walking around this town now. A damned charge like this inflames too many people. They try to take the law in their own hands."

"You didn't believe Reaves, did you?" Rowry couldn't keep the pleading out of his voice.

"Believe that little numskull?" Butler snorted again. "Fat chance. I'm surprised that Judge Chambers reacted as he did. Ordinarily, he wouldn't have issued that charge. No, something's behind this, something we know nothing about." He was silent a moment, then asked, "Does it worry you?"

"It only makes me damned mad," Rowry snapped. "I spent quite a few years working for this town, and its highest official comes up with something like this. Makes a man feel as though all that effort was wasted."

"You know better than that," Butler reproved him. "That's why we've got to dig harder and find out what's behind this. I wish Kilarny would come in. Maybe I'd better go get him."

Rowry shook his head. "It wouldn't do any good. He won't know any more about it than we do."

"I don't know," Butler muttered. "Jeff's got a good head on his shoulders. He might be able to figure what's behind this." He looked up as the door opened. "Speak of the devil," he said, and there was relief in his voice. "We were just talking about you."

"I figured that," Kilarny said dryly. "By the comparison. That's not very flattering, Creed."

"Aw, you know what I meant," Butler growled.

Kilarny grinned, and for an instant, the old, bright expression was back, then his face sobered. "I want to talk to you two."

"Then you've heard what's happened?"

"Biggest topic of conversation in town," Kilarny said. "Who served the charges?"

"Nobody but His Honor himself," Butler grunted. "That doesn't surprise me. That pompous little ass. He was against Rowry ever since the hearing at Inman's death. Maybe this time he sees a better chance to get Rowry. I'm surprised at Judge Chambers. He's too levelheaded to let a wave of hysteria wash him under."

"That surprised me, too," Kilarny said thoughtfully. "Kearns's ugly head hasn't showed yet, but you can bet he's in this someplace. He's a vindictive little snake. He didn't like being beaten at the hearing." He was silent, staring at the far wall. "Rowry, this is going to make you unhappy, but I've got to ask you to tell me all about the fatal night. Rack your brains to see if there's something you left out. No, better go back to the night when those four jumped you and beat the hell out of you."

Rowry groaned, and Kilarny's voice grew stern. "I wouldn't ask you to do this if it wasn't important. Take it slow and put a lot of thought behind each word. Creed, jump in when you think Rowry's overlooking or slighting something. Go ahead, Rowry."

Rowry's face was pained as he started speaking. "On the night they jumped me, they were masked, using grain sack masks with eye and mouth holes cut in them. One of them hit me with a club, and they almost knocked my brains out. They worked me over good and they broke my rifle against a tree. One of them said, 'Maybe you won't make any more cracks about scum.' That gave me the clue to who they were. Ord and I had quarreled about them at suppertime. I ordered him to quit running around with that scum. Ord must've told them what I said, and they decided to knock the hell out of me."

Kilarny looked questioningly at Butler. "He reported this to you?"

"He didn't have to report it," Butler answered. The memory of that night burned in his eyes. "He staggered in here, and he was hurting bad. I got Doc Swanson. Swanson worked on a couple of broken ribs. He wrapped him up like a Christmas package. Rowry crippled around for several weeks before Swanson released him."

Kilarny jotted down some notes as Butler talked. "Why didn't you arrest them? You could have scared a full confession out of them."

"Rowry didn't want me to," Butler said in a disgruntled tone. "He was afraid of what it would do to Sid."

Kilarny glanced at Rowry, and Rowry said in explanation, "Sid had a blind spot where Ord was concerned. He wasn't in the best of health, and I was afraid it would hurt him."

Kilarny nodded his understanding. "But you couldn't just let them go without punishment of any kind?"

Butler chuckled wickedly. "Rowry came up with an idea that sounded good to me. We nipped at those four's butts every time we caught them in town. It got so they were afraid to show their faces. Rowry wanted Ord and the others to squirm good."

Kilarny tapped the pencil against his teeth, and his eyes were thoughtful. "You may have driven them to the bank robbery out of sheer desperation. Maybe it was the only way they saw to get away from your hounding."

Rowry whistled softly. He had never thought of that. "It's a possibility," he said slowly.

"It is," Kilarny agreed. "Now go over the night you shot Ord."

Rowry winced. He didn't want to relive that night, but he started out. He told it slowly, pausing often to think over his words. He finished, and Kilarny said, "The same as you told me this morning."

"Did you expect it to be different?" Rowry asked sourly.

Kilarny grinned. "There could have been a difference. Kearns will nibble at you with his rat teeth. Believe me, he'd catch any discrepancies in your story."

His pencil kept making that clicking sound as he tapped unceasingly on the desk. Kilarny was worried.

"Does something bother you?" Butler asked sharply.

"Something doesn't fit," Kilarny replied. "All Rowry did was what he should be doing. How in the hell could a murder charge be hung on that?"

"You tell us that," Butler snapped.

Kilarny's eyes began to glow, and he looked oddly at Rowry. "Unless there was no robbery at all. Unless Ord was the only one you saw."

Rowry paled, then his cheeks burned. "Are you saying I deliberately made up the story just to get at Ord? Why, goddamn it—"

Kilarny held up a hand to check Rowry. "Whoa! Hold it. That's not my thinking. But it could be someone else's thinking. It would nicely build up that murder charge."

Rowry sucked in his breath, and he felt dizzy. "My God," he said desperately, "I didn't set out deliberately to gun down Ord."

"Stop it," Kilarny commanded. "I told you I don't believe that. And neither does Creed. But something's cooking." He sighed. "We'll just have to wait and see what comes out at the trial."

He stood and tucked his notes into his pocket. "Rowry, I want you to do some more thinking about that night. If anything comes up that you omitted, I want you to send Creed after me. I don't care when it is." He tried to grin and failed miserably. "See you in the morning."

Butler and Rowry sat there a long moment before Rowry spoke. "What do you think, Creed?"

"I don't know," Butler confessed. "Kilarny just had a wild idea. That's all."

"But if that comes out, what will happen?" Rowry persisted.

"Let's don't go jumping at some crazy conclusion," Butler said unhappily. "I'll go out and get you some supper."

"Sure you don't want to lock me up before you leave? I might cut out and run."

"Rowry, you quit horsing around," Butler said bitterly. "I've got enough on my mind as it is."

CHAPTER 16

Rowry's face tightened as he and Butler walked into the courtroom. This was certainly going to be different from the hearing over Inman's shooting. In the first place, the room was packed. Every seat was taken, and people stood in the rear. The murmur of talk grew as Rowry made his way down the aisle toward the front of the court. Rowry felt the back of his neck burn. He tried to avoid staring back at the curious eyes. Was it just normal curiosity in those stares? He couldn't say.

This was different from the hearing in another way: twelve men sat in the jurors' box. Rowry knew every one of them, and several he called close friends. He couldn't say any of them looked friendly now.

He and Butler sat down at a table that a bailiff indicated. Rowry stared straight ahead. He could hear the buzz of excited talk behind him, and it had a menacing sound. If he let his eyes stray to the right, he saw those implacable jurors in the box.

The room grew intolerably hot, and he felt sweat break out on him. "How much longer before this thing starts?" he whispered to Butler.

"It's still a few minutes until nine. Don't let all these curiosity seekers get to you," Butler hissed back.

"They remind me of a bunch of vultures waiting for a body," Rowry growled in a low voice.

He heard a stir of excitement run through the room, and the buzz of talk grew louder. He couldn't resist the temptation to look around. Joe Kearns strolled toward the front of the court, his hair slicked down, an expression of smug confidence on his face. Mayor Reaves followed after him.

"The two chief vultures," Butler remarked. "The feast is about to begin."

In his brief look over his shoulder, Rowry had caught a glimpse of two people, and he wanted to confirm his impression. He deliberately turned, and he was right. Sid sat in the front row, and Abby was only a few seats away from him. Sid's face was set in an unhappy expression. Abby seemed tense.

Their presence was a mild shock to Rowry. He didn't want either of them here.

He mentioned Sid and Abby and asked in a fierce, low voice, "What are they doing here?"

Butler turned his head to confirm Rowry's statement, then shrugged. "I don't know. Maybe Kearns ordered them to be here."

Rowry almost gagged at the thought. "Do you think so?"

Butler's nerves were strung tight, for he snapped, "How do I know? Wait until Kilarny gets here. He may know."

Kearns sat at a similar small table, and Butler glowered at him. Kearns was opening his briefcase and strewing papers about on the table.

"Look at him," Butler growled. "He looks like a mangy tomcat that managed to get into a bowl of cream. God, how I detest that man."

Rowry could agree with Butler, but he had a different feeling about Kearns. His feeling was laced with dread. Kearns seemed so damned positive.

Kilarny came in a few minutes later and sat down at the table with Butler and Rowry. He shook hands with both of them and said, "I guess we've got a full house. I see you got through the night, Rowry."

"Barely," Rowry whispered back. "I didn't know so many hours could be packed in a single night."

Kilarny shook his head sympathetically. "That kind of a night, huh? Anything particular bothering you?"

"Sid and Abby are here." Rowry almost choked over the words. "Why do you think they're here?"

"I can't say about Sid. But I talked to Abby. I told her she might be called. If she was, she was to tell the truth, no matter how rough it sounded for you. I thought Kearns might call her. I suspect he did the same with Sid."

"Everybody stand," the bailiff intoned.

The rustle as the crowd got to their feet seemed deafeningly loud to Rowry. A door behind the bench opened, and Chambers strode through it. He took the bench, standing a moment before he sat down. He was an imposing figure.

"Everybody be seated," the bailiff ordered.

Chambers rapped with his gavel a couple of times, and it caught the full attention of the crowd. "Before we start," Chambers warned, "I want to inform all of you that I will not tolerate any outbreaks in this courtroom." Those steely eyes swept the room.

Rowry felt his throat tighten. This was a different judge from the one at the hearing. Then, Rowry had felt sympathy flowing from the man. There wasn't the slightest vestige of sympathy in Chambers now. His eyes had touched Rowry, then kept on impersonally. It was as though Chambers were looking at a total stranger.

"Read the charges, Bailiff," Chambers ordered.

"The city of Hays, Kansas, against Rowry Saxton. The charge is murder."

"Are you ready, Mr. Kearns?" Chambers asked.

"Ready, Your Honor."

"Then proceed."

"The prosecution intends to prove that Deputy Marshal Saxton deliberately and willfully murdered his brother for no other reason than dislike. Further, we intend to prove—"

Chambers cut him short. Kearns was ready to go into one of his long-winded speeches. "All that can come later. Get on to the business of calling your first witness."

Kearns gulped and said, "Yes, sir. Your Honor, I call Deputy Marshal Saxton to the stand."

Rowry jerked as though a hot needle had been stuck into him. He hadn't expected to be called first. Kilarny reached over and laid a reassuring hand on Rowry's arm. "Easy," he murmured. "Just tell exactly what happened."

Rowry stood and walked to the witness chair. How could just a few paces seem so interminably long? The bailiff swore him in.

Kearns advanced toward him. He reminded Rowry of a feisty terrier stalking an animal that might be more dangerous than he knew. There was a belligerence in him and a caution, too.

"State your name," Kearns said.

"Rowry Saxton." Damn, but his mouth was drying up. He kept swallowing to raise enough saliva to lubricate it.

"Your occupation?"

Rowry glared at him. Kearns knew what he did.

"Answer me," Kearns snapped.

"Deputy marshal of Hays, Kansas," Rowry said sullenly.

"I want you to tell us what happened two nights ago. Tell it exactly as it happened."

Rowry took a moment to gather his thoughts. Was there a warning in Kearns's manner?

"I was patrolling the town," Rowry began. "It was a bad night. It was raining pretty hard, and I was getting wet before I was half-finished."

"Our sympathies for your discomfort," Kearns said sarcastically. "But that's really not what we're interested in. Be more explicit, Deputy."

Rowry glanced at Kilarny. Kilarny briefly shook his head, and Rowry interpreted it rightly. The gesture said, Don't lose your head. "I was approaching the Wellman Bank," he went on. He went ahead relating the events of that fateful night, and his hopes rose as Kearns didn't interrupt him. He must be telling it right. Rowry was particularly careful not to avoid a detail, and he finished with saying, "After two misses at the robbers, I made sure I took enough time with my third shot. I dropped to one knee. The robbers were in a single file. I drew a bead on the last one, and he fell out of the saddle."

"Deputy, you keep saying bank robbery and robbers. Do you want to change that?"

"No," Rowry snapped.

"But you didn't actually see a robbery, did you?"

Rowry shook his head, his stomach tightening. "But I knew one had just happened."

"How did you figure that out?"

"The position of the four, their proximity to the bank, the fact they left their horses in the alley. It was such a bad night, few people even dared venture out."

"But you were out," Kearns purred.

Kilarny was on his feet. "Objection, Your Honor. The prosecutor is badgering the witness."

"Sustained," Chambers snapped. "Mr. Kearns, this isn't a cat and mouse game. If you have anything to say, come to it directly."

"Yes, Your Honor," Kearns said meekly.

He turned back to Rowry, and Rowry thought there was a grin hidden behind that smooth countenance. "Answer my question," he ordered.

"I had to be out. It was my job."

"Did you know who the so-called robber was before you shot?"

Rowry shook his head. "I did not."

"Go ahead," Kearns said shortly.

"I walked over to him and toed the body over."

"How did you know it was a body?"

Rowry flashed an indignant glance at Kilarny, and Kilarny responded by saying, "He's badgering again, Your Honor."

Chambers pointed a finger at Kearns. "I warned you."

Kearns colored. "Your Honor, I'm only trying to find out what happened."

"We'd all like to know that, if you'd only get on with it," Chambers said wearily.

Kearns looked back at Rowry. "Go on."

"I don't know what you want answered."

"How did you know it was a body? Were you so sure of your marksmanship?"

"He fell in that limp, disjointed way that told me he was dead."

Kearns had a comment to make on that, but a glance at Chambers changed his mind. "Go on," he said tersely.

"I toed him over."

"You knew him then?"

Rowry nodded. Now his mouth was so dry he could scarcely speak. "I did. It was Ord Saxton."

Kearns feigned astonishment. "You shot your own brother."

"I didn't know it was my brother when I shot. I shot at a bank robber."

"What would you say if I suggested there was no bank robbery?"

"Are you calling me a liar?" Rowry yelled.

"I'm letting the circumstances do that," Kearns replied.

Chambers banged furiously with his gavel. "I will not have this wrangling in my court," he roared. "Are you saying there was no bank robbery, Mr. Kearns?"

Kearns shook his head, but his eyes glittered. "I was only suggesting the possibility, Your Honor. No more questions. Your witness, Counselor."

Kilarny led Rowry back over the shooting. Just the thought of having to tell it once more sickened him.

"But I told all that," he protested.

"Tell it again," Kilarny said crisply.

Rowry went back over the dreadful sequence, and he was sweating profusely when Kilarny released him.

"Any cross examination?" Chambers asked.

"One or two points I'd like to get firmly fixed in my mind," Kearns said smoothly. He forced Rowry to go through the torture again. He finally finished and said, "No more questions, Your Honor."

Rowry was finally allowed to step down, and his knees felt as though they would buckle and dump him to the floor. He glanced at the clock and couldn't believe what it said. It was almost one o'clock. He had been on that stand nearly four hours.

"He wrung me out like a dishrag," he groaned. He glanced accusingly at Kilarny. "Making me go over that again."

A fleeting grin touched Kilarny's face. "But you didn't waver. Even the third time you went through it."

The bailiff conferred briefly with Chambers, and the judge lifted his head and said, "The bailiff pointed out to me the lateness of the hour. He suggested that I order a recess for lunch. I think it's an excellent suggestion. Court will be recessed until two o'clock."

Butler, Kilarny and Rowry walked out together. "Hungry, Rowry?" Kilarny asked.

Rowry shook his head. Right now he didn't care whether or not he ever ate again.

"You're going to eat," Butler grunted. "You're still taking orders."

Rowry grinned feebly. "What can I do?"

"Not a damned thing," Butler said.

They walked into Ma Atkins' restaurant, and it was crowded. The hum of conversation stopped as the three entered, and heads craned to stare at them.

"If I had any appetite, it's vanished now," Rowry groused.

"You'll eat," Butler said firmly. "None of these curiosity seekers will dare approach our table as long as I'm here."

Ma came over to their table and smiled at them. "How's it going, Rowry?"

"I can't tell," he confessed. "You're busy, aren't you?"

"Snowed under. Usually am on a big trial day. But I'll see to it that you're served." That homely smile flashed again. "It's gonna turn out all right, Rowry. I've got a feeling."

"I hope coming events don't prove your feeling is a liar," Rowry remarked wryly.

Kilarny talked while they waited for service. "I don't know what Kearns is driving at," he said thoughtfully. "That smugness sticks out all over him. He's got some point he wants to make. Did you hear him say maybe there wasn't any robbery at all?"

Rowry moaned. "Hear it? He crammed it down my throat. I was watching the jurors. Their heads came up like a hunting dog when it gets the first scent."

"Creed, I hate to spoil your lunch, but I want you to get out to the scene of the shooting and see if you can find the three shells from Rowry's rifle. I should have thought of that before. Get back here as soon as you can."

Butler nodded without rancor. He only hesitated long enough for Rowry to pinpoint the spot where he stood when he fired. He listened to Rowry, then said, "Got you." He flicked the brim of his hat.

Rowry didn't speak until Butler left the restaurant. "What's Kearns after, Jeff?"

"I wish to God I knew," Kilarny answered and scowled. "When Creed comes back with those shells, maybe it'll help throw a roadblock in front of Kearns. Forget it and eat your lunch. You might need it later."

Rowry could have sworn he couldn't eat at all, but once he got a taste of the food, his appetite built rapidly. "I'm eating like a hog," he apologized.

Kilarny chuckled. "Probably your worry prevented you from eating much before."

Rowry nodded and fell to finishing his food.

Butler came in just as they were finishing. "Rowry, tell me again where you were when the robbers rode out of that alley."

Rowry frowned in concentration. "About fifty yards south of the mouth of that alley. Opposite the bank."

Butler sighed. "I had it right from the start." He stopped and chewed on his lower lip.

"You didn't find the shells," Kilarny said.

"I searched that area real close," Butler said unhappily. "Don't tell me I overlooked it. I knew it was important to you."

Kilarny swore softly. "I should have thought about it the moment I first heard about the shooting from you."

"Don't you believe I told the truth about it?" Rowry asked mournfully.

"Oh, I believe you, all right. But it looks like somebody is trying to kick all the props from under your story. I've got a good hunch that Mr. Kearns had something to do with having those shells picked up." He tapped his fingers restlessly on the table. "Creed, order something. We've got enough time for you to eat."

He sat there in a deep study while Butler ate a hurried meal. "Come up with anything, Jeff?" Butler asked.

"Not a damned thing," Kilarny confessed. "I feel like a blind man trying to find his way around with nothing to guide him. Oh well. It'll come out soon enough. Too soon," he finished grimly.

They ran into Hump Bevins outside the restaurant. Rowry had the feeling Hump had been waiting for them to come out.

"Deputy," Hump drawled. "You know, I'm glad I'm not a friend or a relative of yours." His broad grin displayed bad teeth.

"How's that?" Rowry asked incautiously.

"I'd sure run a good chance of being shot," Hump replied. "First, your so-called friend Inman, then your brother—"

Butler acted before Rowry could even begin to show outrage. He took a quick step forward. "Why, you mouthy bastard," he said. He started the swing as he spoke, and his fist landed as soon as the words were out. It was a powerful blow, one that had the weight of Butler's shoulder and his rage behind it. Bevins groaned, and his eyes rolled up into his head. His knees came unhinged, and he fell flat on his face.

Butler looked thoughtfully at the unmoving form as he rubbed his knuckles.

"Did you think what he said deserved such punishment, Creed?" Kilarny asked.

"I did," Butler said shortly. "I'm getting damned sick of all these so-called judges passing judgment on Rowry. If he doesn't like what I did, let him sue me."

Kilarny shook his head, but he was grinning. "You know, I don't think he will."

They were back in the courtroom before two o'clock. The jury was in its box, and Kilarny glared at Kearns. "Look at him. Did you ever see a more self-satisfied puppy? Whatever he's got in mind, he's satisfied with the way it's going."

The bailiff stood and announced, "Everybody stand."

Chambers entered the room, glanced about, then sat down. "Be seated," he ordered.

The rustle in the room died as everybody took their chairs. "Proceed, Mr. Kearns," Chambers directed.

"I call Sidney Saxton," Kearns called.

Rowry watched his father make his feeble way to the witness chair. Sid looked bad; in fact, he looked far worse than Rowry remembered. His stay at Aunt Edith's house wasn't agreeing with him. Rowry wondered if Sid and Aunt Edith were arguing again.

Sid gave his name at Kearns's direction. "How many sons do you have, Mr. Saxton?"

"I had just one," Sid replied dully.

Kearns's eyebrows arched in surprise. "I thought you had two sons. Ord and Deputy—"

"One," Sid said violently, interrupting him. "My dear son Ord, who is dead. I denounce the other. I consider myself as having one son."

"Ah," Kearns said, flashing a look of triumph at Kilarny. "What do you know about the night of Ord's death?"

"Rowry came home," Sid said in a quavering voice. For a moment, he couldn't go on because he was too choked up.

Kearns waited patiently until Sid got over his spell of weakness.

"Did Rowry have anything to say?" Kearns asked.

"He did," Sid said, his voice going shrill. "He told me he had shot and killed Ord. They had gotten into an argument and Rowry lost his head. He shot—"

Rowry jumped to his feet. "Pa," he screamed. "You're lying."

Chambers pounded with his gavel. "Order in this court," he yelled. He kept pounding his gavel and repeating the words until quiet returned to the room.

Kilarny was frantically pulling at Rowry's arm. "Rowry," he hissed. "You're only making matters worse."

"I don't care," Rowry shouted. "He's lying. I told him everything that happened that night."

"Another such outbreak, and you'll be fined for contempt of court," Chambers roared.

That got through to Rowry. He was in bad enough trouble without adding a contempt fine to it. He sat down and said stubbornly in a lower voice, "He's lying."

"I know he is," Kilarny replied. "But I'll take care of him. Our time will come."

Kearns couldn't keep his smug grin from showing. "You're sure, Mr. Saxton, that Rowry didn't say anything about a bank robbery?"

"No, he didn't," Sid declared. He threatened to break down again, and Kearns gave him time to recover. "Rowry was always picking on poor Ord. Ord was a gentle, sweet boy."

Rowry made a retching sound in his throat.

Kearns asked a couple of further questions, then said, "Your witness, Counselor."

Kilarny approached Sid, and Sid's eyes were wary. He shrank back as far as he could into his chair.

"Mr. Saxton," Kilarny said gently. "Are you sure you don't want to change any of your testimony?"

Sid shook his head vigorously. "I ain't got anything to change. Everything I said was gospel truth."

Kilarny's tone changed. It crackled like distant thunder. "Mr. Saxton, do you realize that lying under oath is a serious crime? A person can be punished severely for lying in the witness chair."

Kearns was on his feet. "Your Honor, Mr. Kilarny is intimidating the witness, an old man at that."

"Sustained," Chambers said wearily. "Mr. Kilarny, you know better than that. Don't make me warn you again."

Kilarny looked injured. "Your Honor, it's my belief that this witness is lying."

"Then bring it out in proper testimony," Chambers snapped.

Kilarny went back to Sid. "You say Ord was a gentle, sweet boy? Hardworking, too?"

Sid nodded again. "Always at something every minute of the day."

"Where did he work? Careful, Mr. Saxton. This can be verified. Where did he work?" he thundered.

Sid licked his lips and threw a look at Kearns, but Kearns couldn't help him. Sid took so long that Chambers instructed him, "Answer the question, Mr. Saxton."

"Who was he working for?" Kilarny repeated.

Sid tried to think of something and came up empty. "He wasn't working right now," he said hesitantly.

"But you just said he was a hardworking boy, working every minute of the day. Wasn't that a kind of lying, Mr. Saxton?"

Kearns was on his feet again. "Your Honor—" he started.

"Sit down," Chambers said wearily. "Mr. Kilarny is well within his rights. Proceed, Mr. Kilarny."

"Weren't you lying?" Kilarny asked in that crackling voice.

"Maybe I did," Sid mumbled. "I didn't want folks to get the wrong impression of my boy."

"How long has it been since he worked?" Kilarny went on relentlessly. "Come on, Mr. Saxton. Surely you remember when your boy last worked." He looked at Sid's reddening face and pointed a finger at him. "Was it so far back that you can't even remember? Or maybe he's never worked. Name two places he's worked in all of his life."

"He worked for me," Sid said shrilly. "He did everything I asked him to do."

"That hardly counts, Mr. Saxton," Kilarny said dryly. "Then wouldn't you say that Ord wasn't a hardworking boy?"

"That's only your opinion," Sid said viciously. "I got my own—"

"That's all, Mr. Saxton," Kilarny cut him short. He turned a contemptuous back on a beaten old man.

He rejoined Rowry and Butler at the table. "I know I was hard on him," he said to Rowry. "But, my God, he deserved that."

"He sure as hell did," Butler agreed.

"Jeff, I'm not blaming you. You're fighting for me." But inwardly Rowry was sick. He was sorry for an ill old man, then reason took over. Sid shouldn't have lied in the first place. Kilarny had at least put a doubt in the minds of the listeners. Ord wasn't the paragon of virtue that Sid had tried to paint him.

"I call Abby Barnett," Kearns said.

Rowry jerked as though he had been stung. He cast imploring eyes at Kilarny.

"Easy," Kilarny said soothingly. "Kearns will probably call anybody in town who has the slightest knowledge of you." He grinned steadily, though a worry ran through his mind. There wouldn't be much he could do about tearing apart Abby's testimony. That wouldn't set well with the judge and the jurors.

Abby gave her name and her occupation after she sat down. Her head was held high and her face was composed.

"Do you know Deputy Saxton?" Kearns asked.

"I know him," she said in a soft voice.

"How well?" Kearns insisted.

"Very well," she answered crisply. "We've been going together for the last two years."

"But you didn't approve of some of the things he did," Kearns suggested.

"What things?" she demanded.

Kilarny grinned. "I think Kearns has stepped into a bumblebee nest and is just beginning to realize it. You can sit back and enjoy this, Rowry. I'd hate to try to twist that gal's mind around."

"Such as the way he treated his brother," Kearns floundered.

"Rowry didn't come down on Ord hard enough," she stated firmly. "Ord was a constant source of worry to Rowry. He talked about it often."

Kearns was getting in deeper, and he didn't know how to back out. "Why was he worried, Miss Barnett?"

"He worried about Ord not working and about his drinking. Sid had no influence on Ord, and Rowry couldn't make him listen to anything."

"Beautiful, beautiful," Kilarny murmured. "This is one place where Kearns outsmarted himself."

"But Deputy Saxton hated Ord, didn't he?"

"He did not," Abby lashed back. "He cared for his brother, or he wouldn't have worried so much."

Kearns said unhappily, "Your witness, Mr. Kilarny."

"Did you know Ord well, Miss Barnett?" Kilarny asked.

"I knew him." Distaste was in her voice.

"Through Rowry's eyes or your own?"

"My own," she answered. "Several times, I've heard Rowry trying to make Ord listen to reason. He got nowhere. Ord was a spoiled kid. He was only twenty. Rowry knew that, and he hoped Ord would grow out of his willfulness."

"That's all," Kilarny said. "Thank you."

She stepped down from the witness chair, her head high, and retook her seat.

Kearns called one witness after another. It seemed as though he were intent on calling half of the town. Every witness was almost a duplicate of the preceding one. Ord was a good kid, hardworking and unselfish. His loss was a terrible blow to the town.

At four o'clock, Chambers asked wearily, "How long does this go on, Mr. Kearns?"

"I don't understand your question, sir."

"How many witnesses do you intend to call who will testify in a like manner?"

"I'm only trying to prove how valuable Ord was to this community," Kearns protested.

"I'd say you've proven or disproven it enough," Chambers said dryly. "The hour is growing late. Court adjourned until tomorrow morning at nine." He stood and walked out of the room.

Kilarny, Butler and Rowry waited until the room emptied. "Jeff, how do you think we came out?" Rowry asked anxiously.

"Pretty well," Kilarny answered cautiously. "Sid did Kearns no good, and Abby almost wrecked him. All that list of witnesses didn't help him, either."

"I don't see why not," Rowry said morosely. "All every damned one of them did was sing Ord's praises."

"Aha," Kilarny said knowingly. "But you didn't pay any attention to the caliber of those witnesses."

Butler leaned forward. "What do you mean by that?"

"Was there a solid citizen among them, Creed?"

Butler gave that some thought, then said slowly, "By golly, you're right. Every one of them belonged to the shiftless, the ne'er-do-wells. Jeff, do you think they were handpicked?"

"It's something to think about," Kilarny replied. "Ready to go?"

They walked out of the courtroom, and Rowry turned down the offer of a meal at Ma Atkins' restaurant. "I might run into another Hump," he said and tried to grin.

"Go on back to the jail," Butler said. "I'll bring you something."

"Aren't you going to lock me up?" Rowry asked.

"Don't try to be funny," Butler said sourly.

"I can't go," Kilarny said. "I have to talk to the Edison and Duncan families tonight. It's odd that Dent and Chad didn't show up at the trial. I'd like to find out where those two are."

"Why not Wellman?" Butler asked.

"To ask about Verl?" Kilarny shook his head. "Wellman wouldn't say anything anyway. Somehow, I don't trust that man."

"Two of us," Butler said, and his laughter had a nasty ring.

CHAPTER 17

Rowry and Butler got down to the courthouse ten minutes before nine, but Kilarny was there waiting for them.

"Sit down," he said, his eyes sparkling with renewed interest. "I talked to Mr. Edison and Mr. Duncan last night."

"Find out anything interesting?" Butler asked.

Kilarny nodded solemnly. "At first, neither of them wanted to talk to me. I threatened them mildly, and they opened up a little. I got the feeling they were evading something. You know how it is when a man won't look straight at you. You get the feeling he's lying and trying to cover up."

"Then it didn't do you any good," Rowry said in disappointment.

"It did," Kilarny corrected him. "Mr. Edison told me that Dent is out of town, visiting his grandmother in Kansas City. Probably will be gone all summer."

"Go on," Rowry said, breathing harder.

"I had the same trouble getting Duncan to talk. I finally managed to pry out of him that Chad is visiting his aunt in Abilene. Might be a long visit of two or three months." He shook his head impatiently as Rowry's face didn't light up. "Don't you understand? Both boys being out of town at the same time visiting relatives is too pat. I have a conviction that if Wellman could be made to talk, Verl would also be visiting out of town." His eyes clouded. "There's a plot brewing. And I don't like the smell of it."

"What do you think it is, Jeff?" Rowry asked.

"I'm scared to say what I've got in mind, Rowry. We'll just have to see how it works out."

Kearns came in, flashing them a triumphant glance. It was almost time for the court to start. Kilarny watched him with hawk eyes. "He seems so damned sure of himself," he murmured.

The courtroom was again filled. This was the most interesting trial that had hit Hays in several years. Everybody stood as Chambers came in. He took a moment to instruct Kearns. "Mr. Kearns, I will not have a repeat of yesterday afternoon. Is that understood?"

Kearns flushed, but he didn't raise his eyes from the floor. "It is, Your Honor," he said in a reedy voice. "I call Mr. Parker."

Kilarny threw Rowry a puzzled look, and Rowry said, "Jim isn't much more than a bum."

Parker took the witness chair, and he was on the seedy side. He needed a haircut, and no one could call him clean-shaven.

Kearns went through the usual procedure. "Your business, Mr. Parker."

Parker cleared his throat. "I closed up my business a couple of years back. Health, you know."

"Did you know Ord Saxton?"

Parker's face brightened. "I'll say I did. I couldn't have thought more of my own son. He worked for me for several years. Bright, industrious boy. Always willing to put out more effort than any other two boys."

"Kearns is trying to rebuild Ord's reputation," Kilarny whispered to Rowry. "My God, what a fraud. I'm surprised that Chambers allows it."

Kearns finished his questioning and turned the witness over to Kilarny. Kilarny asked casually, "You say you knew Ord Saxton well?"

"I sure did," Parker said, bobbing his head. "Best worker I ever had."

"When was that, Mr. Parker?"

Parker's face furrowed in heavy thought. "I said I had to retire some years back. My heart isn't too good."

"Wasn't that retirement almost eight years ago, Mr. Parker?"

Parker blinked.

Butler had filled in Kilarny well. "Isn't it true that the business you opened lasted less than a year?" Kilarny pounded at him relentlessly. "You went broke."

"It wasn't my fault," Parker said indignantly. "I ran into a couple of cheats. I didn't know until—"

"Enough," Kilarny said wearily. "You haven't worked since you retired?"

"I told you my—"

Kilarny nodded and interrupted him. "I know about your heart. Have you worked since then?"

"I would have if I could," Parker said virtuously. "But I'm getting stronger. Another few weeks—"

"Let's get back to the subject under discussion," Kilarny snapped. "You said Ord worked for you. And it's been eight years since you closed your doors."

"I tried to tell you it wasn't my fault," Parker whined.

"Oh, stop it," Kilarny flashed out. "Wouldn't that have made Ord twelve years old? I believe you said he worked for you for several years. How old was he when he started?"

Parker blinked several times, then said sullenly, "I told you Ord worked for me. If you don't want to believe it, that's your business. I ain't answering any more questions."

Kilarny grinned wolfishly. "You don't have to, Mr. Parker. You've answered enough one way or the other. No more questions, Your Honor."

Chambers dismissed the witness, and Parker shambled back to his original chair. He shook his head as he passed Kearns, and it was an eloquent gesture.

"That sanctimonious old liar," Kilarny said heatedly. "I'm surprised that the judge allows Kearns to go on like he has. What's he going to pull next?"

Kearns called Dobie Eagan next, and Kilarny looked inquiringly at Butler.

"An odd-jobman around town. Never very permanent or too reliable. When Dobie gets a few dollars together, he drinks them up. My God, do you think Kearns is going to try and pull the same thing?"

"Bet on it," Kilarny said. His eyes danced. How he was enjoying this clash of minds.

Eagan stated his name and his occupation. "I got no regular business," he said piously. "Maybe some people might look down on what I do, but I'm telling you this town would get in a hell of a shape if I wasn't around to keep things running."

"Did Ord work for you?"

"Whenever he had the opportunity. I gave him all the work I

could. Never saw a harder-working kid. We just finished a job not over a month ago. I'm gonna miss Ord."

"I can't believe it," Kilarny whispered. "I'm surprised Chambers allows this to go on." He advanced toward Eagan after Kearns said, "Your witness, Counselor."

"Mr. Eagan," Kilarny said solicitously. "I'll bet in your line of work, you've known some hard days."

"That I have, sir. After some of the days I put in, I didn't think I'd be able to cripple back home."

Kilarny feigned sympathy. "Where was this last job you mentioned? The one you said Ord worked with you?"

Eagan squirmed. "I can't remember," he said evasively. "My memory ain't as good as it used to be."

"But you know that Ord worked for you." A new toughness had entered Kilarny's voice.

"I remember names and people," Eagan said indignantly.

"Fine," Kilarny approved. "What was the people's names you worked for?" He pretended shock as Eagan shook his head. "You can't remember that, either? What kind of a job was it?"

Eagan shook his head again.

"Isn't that amazing?" Kilarny lashed out. "Apparently the only thing you can remember about this whole sorry matter is Ord's name." He turned toward the bench. "Your Honor, I suggest this witness is lying, just as more than a few witnesses before have done. I'd hate to think that those witnesses are a good representation of Hays."

"I'm inclined to agree with your conclusion, Mr. Kilarny," Chambers said dryly. "The witness is dismissed. Mr. Kearns, will you approach the bench?"

He tongue-lashed Kearns for the low caliber of his witnesses, and Kearns said defensively, "How would I know that, Your Honor? I asked for people who were familiar with Ord Saxton, and the ones you heard are the ones I got."

"Didn't it strike you as odd that that kind were the only ones to respond?" Chambers didn't wait for Kearns's reply but leaned over the bench, his face frozen and foreboding. "This is my last warning, Mr. Kearns. If your next witness isn't reputable—"

"He will be, Your Honor," Kearns said hastily. "I call Mr. Wellman."

Eyebrows rose all over the room, and Kilarny said, "Here it comes. The ace Kearns has had up his sleeve."

Wellman took the chair and looked out over the audience. His eyes were hooded in that long, horsey face; his appearance was chilling.

"Your occupation, Mr. Wellman."

Wellman glared at Kearns. "You know what I do."

"Please, sir," Kearns said. "The court must know."

"I own and run the biggest bank in Hays," Wellman said disdainfully.

"Was there a robbery at your bank a couple of nights ago, the night of the big rain?"

Wellman snorted. "My bank hasn't known a robbery in the last ten years."

The collective sucking in of breaths ran through the room.

"Are you sure, Mr. Wellman?" Kearns asked in astonishment. "Deputy Saxton says he broke one up. He said four men—"

"I know what he said," Wellman interrupted. "Deputy Saxton is a liar."

Kilarny glanced at Rowry and nodded grimly. "Now everything is out in the open," he said quietly.

"Would you explain that, Mr. Wellman?" Mr. Kearns asked.

"Deputy Saxton was in a bind. He had to have a reason to cover up shooting his own brother."

Rowry wanted to charge Wellman, and he would have risen if Kilarny hadn't reached out and seized his arm.

"Mr. Wellman, I want to warn you of the gravity of your statement," Kearns said.

Wellman snorted again. "I only know what I saw."

"Would you describe what you saw to the court?"

"I'll be happy to. I had worked late that night and was just stepping out of the front door. Ord passed me and said a pleasant goodnight. I wondered why he was going out on that kind of a night, but I didn't ask him. I had other things on my mind."

He paused in reflection, and Kearns prompted him. "Yes, Mr. Wellman."

Those eyes were glittering in that cold, impassive face. "Ord had just passed the alley when I saw Deputy Saxton on the other side of the street and some distance behind."

The courtroom was completely hushed, hanging on every word. "Yes, Mr. Wellman?" Kearns urged him on.

"The deputy didn't call out to Ord or warn him by any sign. He dropped to one knee, and I saw his rifle come up. The crack of that rifle was more shocking than a clap of thunder. I was so stunned I couldn't move. Saxton turned and moved away."

"He didn't even go up to see how badly his brother was hurt?"

Wellman shrugged. "I guess he knew by the way Ord fell."

"What did you do?"

"I went up to Ord and bent over him. He was dead, all right. I was in a quandary, not knowing exactly what to do. I did go over to the spot where the deputy had kneeled to fire. I found this." He reached into his pocket and pulled out a single shell.

Kearns took it and bounced it in his hand. "But the deputy said he fired three times."

Wellman's laugh had a brittle ring. "I know what he said. But that was the only shell I found."

Again that long pause, and Kearns prodded him again. "Go on, Mr. Wellman."

"I heard some men coming down the street. I didn't know who they were, but they were sure to find Ord's body. I didn't want any further involvement in this distasteful matter. I turned and went on home."

"Is there anything you want to add, Mr. Wellman?"

Wellman thought for a moment. "I agonized for quite a while, then I knew I couldn't let it pass. I came to your office and talked it over with you. You advised me to testify openly in court. I decided to follow your advice." Wellman raised his hands and let them fall.

There was nasty, open triumph in Kearns's eyes as he said, "Your witness, Mr. Kilarny."

"He's a goddamned liar," Rowry whispered passionately. He couldn't see Abby's face, but he knew the shock that must be on it.

"We know that," Kilarny said assuringly. "Now we're going to have to drag it out in the open for everybody to see."

He advanced toward Wellman, his face truculent. "Do you insist that what you said was the truth, Mr. Wellman?"

Wellman looked disdainfully at him. "I am not in the habit of lying, Mr. Kilarny. Anybody who's dealt with me is well aware of that."

Rowry watched the jurors' faces. He couldn't read any of them well enough to know how they were accepting this electrifying change. God, let Kilarny be at his best, he thought.

"Why do you suppose Deputy Saxton shot his brother?" Kilarny asked.

Again Wellman shrugged. "How would I know? Maybe some ancient quarrel between them had festered so much that the deputy couldn't stand it any longer. He picked a night when he was sure nobody would be around. Unfortunately for him, I was."

Kilarny cocked his head, studying him. "Do you know what I think, Mr. Wellman? I think you're lying in your teeth."

Kearns was instantly on his feet, screaming his objection. "He has no right to say anything like that, Your Honor."

"Sustained," Chambers thundered. "Counselor, do you want to withdraw that statement?"

Kilarny's twisted smile had an appealing cast to it. "I withdraw the statement, Your Honor. I'm afraid I was presumptuous."

"You were," Chambers said severely. "See that it doesn't happen again."

Kilarny nodded. He changed his tactics and asked, "Mr. Wellman, where is Verl at the moment?"

Kearns was once more on his feet, screaming his objection. "That question isn't pertinent to the matter at hand."

Wellman answered before Chambers could speak. "I don't mind answering that question. Verl is in New Orleans, visiting his uncle. He's been gone a couple of weeks and expects to be there all summer. He's been looking forward to that trip for a long time. He hasn't been in New Orleans before."

Kilarny stood before him, pityingly shaking his head. "Do you want me to tell what really happened, Mr. Wellman?"

Wellman looked suddenly wary, and his cheeks were hollowed. "I don't care what you say. I know where Verl is."

"Isn't it odd that Verl and Chad Duncan and Dent Edison should pick the same time to be out of town?"

Wellman's jaw thrust forward belligerently. "I don't know where Chad and Dent are. I only know about Verl."

"Those boys were pretty close, weren't they?" Kilarny asked. "Everybody in town knew of their attachment. They were seen together every place in town."

"I guess they were pretty close," Wellman admitted cautiously. "Just a boyhood attachment. They'd grow out of it."

"Ord made the fourth of that group, didn't he?" Kilarny asked softly.

Wellman shifted restlessly, and his face lost some of its former color. "Maybe he was," he said slowly. "A few times."

"They were inseparable," Kilarny thundered. "Where one was seen, the other three were there. Did you know that Ord hated his brother? They quarreled frequently, mostly about the gang he ran around with."

"I didn't know any of that." Wellman's voice was beginning to show strain.

"Rowry tried to make Ord break with his associates. Not too far back he and Ord quarreled about it. Rowry made a disparaging remark about running around with scum. Ord didn't like it. He told the other three about it, and they took out their abused feelings on Rowry. They jumped him that night."

Kearns was on his feet again. "None of this has been brought out before," he bawled. "Your Honor, this is inadmissible."

"I'll decide that," Chambers said severely. "Mr. Kilarny, why wasn't any of this brought out before?"

"I was hoping to save Ord's father's feelings from being hurt. But now I am forced to bring it up."

"Then you better call other witnesses to substantiate that."

Kilarny nodded his agreement. "I call Deputy Saxton."

Rowry groaned. He didn't want to be in that chair again. He took the chair and told of the sneak attack as fluently as he could. "The four jumped me from an alley. All four were masked with makeshift masks made out of grain sacks. One of them used a club and damned near knocked me out. They beat on me pretty good."

Chambers leaned forward, his interest completely aroused. "If they were masked, how did you know it was the four we've just talked about?"

"One of them repeated my remark about the scum Ord was running around with. Then he kicked me. He damned near busted two of my ribs."

"Is there anybody else who can substantiate this story?" Chambers asked.

"Yes, sir," Kilarny answered. "I call Marshal Butler."

Butler had to take the oath, for he hadn't been in the chair before. "Marshal, do you remember the night Rowry was talking about?"

"I sure as hell do," Butler replied. "He came staggering in and barely made it to a chair. His face was a mess. If I ever looked at a man hurting bad, I was looking at one. I sent for Doctor Swanson. I don't see him at the trial, but he can verify what I'm saying."

"If it's necessary, we'll send for him," Kilarny commented. "Go on."

"I wanted to arrest them, and Rowry talked me out of it. I asked if he intended to just let them go without punishment of any kind. He said he had an idea that might straighten out Ord. At the very least, it would scare the hell out of him and the others." He grinned. "We rousted those four real good. Every time we caught them in town, we ran them out." He chuckled at the memory. "It got so that those four kids took off at the very sight of us. The last couple of weeks before the bank robbery, we didn't see them at all. Rowry told me after he reported the robbery that we may have driven the four to it." That wolf grin appeared again. "It was entirely possible," he finished softly.

"You're talking about the same four that Rowry saw during the robbery."

"I am," Butler said crisply.

"Name them, Marshal."

Butler nodded. "Verl Wellman, Chad Duncan and Dent Edison. And the dead one, Ord Saxton."

"That'll do, Marshal."

Kilarny waited until Butler stepped down, then said, "I call Abby Barnett."

She took the stand, her composure unruffled.

"Do you know anything about this, Miss Barnett?"

Abby nodded. "Rowry came by the night after he was so badly beaten. He had trouble moving. He told me he suspected the four Marshal Butler named. He said he wasn't going to do anything about it except to try and scare some sense into Ord's head. He was worried about Mr. Saxton's health. He hadn't been in the best of health."

"Thank you, Miss Barnett. Any questions, Counselor?"

Kearns looked absolutely beaten. "No questions," he mumbled.

"Any more witnesses?" Chambers asked.

Kilarny shook his head. "I have no more witnesses."

Chambers summed up the salient points. "In many ways, this has been an extremely odd case. You listened to facts and, I'm afraid, quite a few lies. It's your duty to sift the facts from the lies and judge them. Did a robbery take place, or was it a clever defense to hide a man's guilt? All of you know the principals in this case very well. Which do you put the most trust in? The jury will adjourn to the jury room. Talk it over there, then return to announce your decision."

Rowry watched the jury file out of the box, and he could feel the sour sickness rising in his throat. Everything he had was hanging on the coming decision; his job, his freedom, maybe even his life depended upon what those twelve men decided.

"Jeff," he said hollowly. "I'm scared."

"That makes two of us," Kilarny said gravely. "Nobody can tell which way a jury will go. But every one of those men knows you, Rowry, and your reliability. I think you can depend on that."

Rowry tried to grin and failed. "I haven't got anything else to depend on," he said in a squeaky voice.

Time slowly ticked away. Every time Rowry glanced at the clock, he could swear neither hand had moved. The passage of time wore on his nerves. "My God, Jeff," he said, trying to keep his voice normal. "They've been out almost two hours."

Kilarny grinned, and a sparkle had returned to his eyes. "They've got a big problem to solve, Rowry. I hope they stay out longer. It means they're not in agreement. Some of those twelve men must believe you're not a liar."

Kilarny's words were consoling, but they didn't help the ache in Rowry's head. Those inexorable crawling hands had reached a quarter of six when Chambers said impatiently, "Bailiff, go see if the jury is close to a decision. Tell them if they don't reach one by six o'clock, they'll be locked up for the night."

The bailiff was almost at the jury room door when it opened and the jury filed out.

"They're coming out, Your Honor," the bailiff said.

"I can see," Chambers said testily. He waited until the jury was seated, then asked, "Has the jury reached a decision?"

God, Rowry's temples ached so that he thought somebody was beating on them with a maul. He was going to hear the fateful words that gave him freedom or locked him up, or worse.

Ben Carter, the foreman of the jury, stood. He was a lanky man with bowed shoulders, and his face was unhappy. "We have not, Your Honor. We were just coming out to tell you so."

"How does the decision stand now?" Chambers asked.

"Split right down the middle," Carter groaned. "All the reasoning in the world couldn't change those hard heads. I'm afraid it's useless, Your Honor. If you locked us up for the rest of our lives, I believe the decision would be the same."

"Are you certain more deliberation will do no good?"

Carter grimaced. "I'm positive, sir."

Chambers sighed and said, "Then I see only one thing to do—dismiss the jury."

Kearns was on his feet, screaming his objection. "You can't do that, Judge," he bawled. "It would be an absolute miscarriage of justice."

Chambers frowned at him. "What would you suggest I do?"

"Schedule this case for another trial." Kearns was so shaken he was almost babbling.

"You know that's impossible," Chambers snapped. "Rowry cannot be tried twice for the same crime. Case dismissed."

CHAPTER 18

Kilarny, Butler and Rowry sat and waited while people filed out of the courtroom. "Why so glum, Rowry?" Kilarny asked. "You look like you've lost your last friend. Don't you realize you're a free man? You beat a clever case set up against you. It could just as easily have gone the other way."

"I don't feel like I've got a friend in the world," Rowry said moodily. "You heard what Carter said. They were split right down the middle. That means half of them believed I was guilty."

Kilarny grinned. "Look at the other side. Half of them believed you were innocent."

"That's not very encouraging," Rowry growled. "Half of the town must figure that I'm a liar and a murderer."

"That's about the right percentage," Kilarny said thoughtfully. "You take any question of importance, and a split is about the best you can do."

Rowry stubbornly shook his head. "It won't do for me. Every time I see someone looking at me, I'll wonder what's behind his eyes."

"Oh hell," Butler said in disgust. "He not only isn't satisfied with winning, he wants recommendations from the entire town. We can clear out now. Ready to go?"

"Might as well," Kilarny answered. "Hungry tonight, Rowry?"

Rowry shook his head. "Not very."

"Give up on him, Jeff," Butler said. "You can't satisfy him."

Rowry grinned wryly. "I didn't say my proper thanks, Jeff. Without you, you'd know where I'd be."

"I can guess," Kilarny said.

Rowry shivered as the nightmare returned. It would be a long time before he could stop thinking of those two days.

"Six o'clock stage's just in," Butler announced. "A little late. Want to go see who came in on it?"

Rowry shrugged. It didn't make any difference to him one way or the other.

The stage was packed, and the three stood and watched the passengers descend. "Why, that's Dan Edmonds," Rowry exclaimed as the short, pudgy figure stepped down to the ground. "Dan," he called. "I thought you were finished here. What's bringing you back?"

Edmonds looked nervously at Butler and Kilarny. "I had to return, Rowry. I read about your case. I had to go to Russell on my next assignment, but I was worrying how you were coming out. I had to come back."

Rowry introduced him to Butler and Kilarny. "Jeff was my lawyer," he said. "I'd be in real trouble if it hadn't been for him."

Kilarny had been studying the nervous agitation of the short man, and he asked, "Mr. Edmonds, were you examining the Wellman Bank during the trial?"

"Only the first day," Edmonds replied. "I finished up before the trial ended. I couldn't keep my mind on my work."

"Why?" Kilarny asked gently.

"It isn't ethical to tell you what I know," Edmonds said, running a finger inside his collar. "But I found something highly irregular. I don't know whether or not it'd be helpful to Rowry." He hesitated and licked his lips.

"It could be of the utmost importance," Kilarny said, his voice firm. "If Rowry's a friend of yours, tell him."

Edmonds grinned shakily. "I consider him one of the best I have. I owe him something. He saved me from being run down by a runaway horse. Maybe this will repay a little of my debt."

Kilarny shook his head at Rowry, a barely discernible gesture that said, Let him tell this at his own pace.

Edmonds was still struggling with his conscience, and Kilarny tried to help him. "Was the Wellman Bank robbed, Mr. Edmonds?" he asked bluntly.

Edmonds shook his head. "No, nothing like that. The books were all in order. But there was an irregularity that kept bothering me. Mr. Wellman had taken eleven thousand dollars out of his personal account and deposited it with the bank's funds."

"Ah," Kilarny said, his eyes shining. "Did he explain that to you?"

"I demanded that he do so," Edmonds said stoutly. "He said he had borrowed the money from the bank to take care of an advantageous deal that came up. He had returned the money to the bank as soon as he could."

"That was irregular," Kilarny commented.

"I know it," Edmonds said vigorously. "I reproved him sternly. He promised me it would never happen again. He talked so convincingly that I said I wouldn't report it." He wiped a shaky hand across his brow. "Is this going to be helpful to Rowry?"

Kilarny seized his hand and pumped it. "You don't know how much, Mr. Edmonds. Rowry will be eternally grateful."

Edmonds blew out a relieved breath. "Then I can return to Russell with a clear conscience. I've just got time to catch the returning stage. I can get back to my work with an untroubled conscience."

He shook hands all around, then hurried inside the stage depot to purchase a ticket.

"Talk about casting your bread upon the waters," Kilarny exclaimed. His voice had a new ring that hadn't been there before.

"What's this all about?" Rowry asked bewilderedly.

"Don't you get it?" Kilarny asked impatiently. "That old hypocrite. Don't you see, Rowry? There was a robbery at Wellman's bank. Wellman transferred his personal funds to cover the robbery. He was trying to save his son from paying the price of his crime. Damn it, if I had only known this during the trial."

"Things would have been different?" Butler asked.

"Rowry, you would have been completely cleared, without suspicion or blame from a single person. Wellman and Kearns worked this up together. That damned Kearns. I'll bet he picked up a neat sum for his services."

"You know it, but what good is it going to do?" Butler asked practically. "How are you going to go about proving it?"

"I'll prove it," Kilarny stated. "I feel like a new man, and I'm hungry. How about it now, Rowry?"

"I'm suddenly hungry," Rowry said, a new glow in his eyes. "I can eat a horse." They fell into stride as they walked toward Ma

Atkins' restaurant. "One thing still sticks in my mind. How will you prove it? You don't expect Wellman to admit it?"

"No way," Kilarny said decisively. "But Charley Tucker still works for the bank. He's an old man. I imagine he's scared about the burden he's been carrying around. The bank's closed for the day. I can't talk to Charley until in the morning."

"I want to be there when you question him," Butler growled.

"I don't see that it would do any harm," Kilarny decided. "It might increase the pressure on Tucker." His eyes were dancing; he looked like the Kilarny of old. "Come on. I'm like Rowry—I could eat a horse. Let's get on down there before that horse is all gone."

CHAPTER 19

Kilarny stood across the street from the Wellman Bank, his face growing unhappier with each passing minute. He had seen Charley Tucker open the bank promptly at nine, and he had hoped to follow him in a moment after. It was now nine-thirty, and Butler still wasn't here. Kilarny swore under his breath. He would give Butler ten more minutes, then take care of this by himself. He wished now he hadn't agreed to Butler's coming with him, but last night he had promised. At the time, it had seemed a good idea. Butler's presence and his badge might be just enough additional pressure to make Tucker babble like a ten-year-old.

Damn it, Creed, he thought. If you delay much longer, Wellman will be down, and he'd be enough to strengthen the old man. Kilarny doubted that Tucker would say anything harmful to Wellman if Wellman were around.

He muttered a final oath as he saw Butler hurrying down the street. It was about time. Butler had to be in the last minute of the ten Kilarny had allowed him.

"I thought we agreed on nine o'clock," he said sharply.

"I know it, Jeff," Butler apologized. "But I couldn't help it. Snead

got drunk and was beating up his wife. Her screams roused the
neighbors, and they came after me. I had to stop that, didn't I?"

"I suppose so," Kilarny muttered. "What did you do with Snead?"

"He's locked up," Butler said savagely. "This is the second time
I've had to do it. Maybe a longer stay will teach him something."

"It didn't teach Inman," Kilarny reminded him. "Why didn't you
send Rowry?"

"I couldn't." An unhappy scowl crossed Butler's face. "I told
Rowry to come in late this morning. He'd spent the last three nights
sleeping on that jail cot. That cot isn't the most comfortable thing in
the world. He wasn't down when I left. Did you see Wellman come
in?" At Kilarny's shaking head, he said practically, "Then there's no
harm done. Charley's still alone, isn't he?"

"I suppose so," Kilarny replied. "Let's get it over with."

They crossed the street and walked into the bank. There were no
customers, and that was all to their good. They approached Tucker
in his teller's cage. His head was down as he wrestled with some
figures.

Kilarny cleared his throat, and the sound jerked up Tucker's head.
"Good morning, gentlemen," he said, his voice sounding a little
strained. "What can I do for you?"

Kilarny noticed that Tucker's eyes had flicked from him to Butler,
resting longer on the marshal.

"Hello, Charley," he said softly. "We're not here on business. The
more important question is what can we do for you. You could be in
serious trouble, Charley."

Charley gulped, and his Adam's apple showed plainly in his
throat. "What do you mean, 'I could be in trouble'?" His voice was
little stronger than a squeak.

"For not reporting a bank robbery when it happened, Charley,"
Kilarny said. "The marshal here is mighty interested in your negli-
gence."

Charley went rigid, and there was pure fright in those wild, staring
eyes. All the color vanished from his face.

"A bank robbery," he stammered. "I don't know what you mean."

"I think you do," Kilarny said with cruel intentness. "It didn't
happen too far back. It was on the night of the big rain. The penalty

for conspiring to cover up a crime would go hard on an old man like you. You might not live long enough to ever see your freedom again."

Tucker closed his eyes and swayed back and forth. Both Kilarny and Butler thought he was going to faint. Only a quick grab at the edge of the counter saved him.

"Of course, it could go easier on you if you worked with us," Kilarny purred. "If you told us about it now."

Tucker's reaction was certainly not what he expected. Tucker opened his mouth and screamed at the top of his lungs. "Mr. Wellman, Mr. Wellman," he screamed. "You'd better get out here in a hurry."

Wellman came dashing out of his office, and his face was startled and angry at the same time. "What's going on out here?" he roared.

"Mr. Wellman, these two are in here accusing me of knowing about a bank robbery."

There was a tightening of the skin at the corners of Wellman's eyes. "What did you tell them?" he asked cautiously.

"What could I tell them, Mr. Wellman? I didn't hear about any robberies. How could I when there was no robbery at this bank?"

Wellman's color returned to normal. He glared at Kilarny and Butler. "It's a good thing I had to get down here early this morning. If I hadn't been here, there's no telling how bad you would have scared this old man."

"Even into telling us about the robbery?" Kilarny asked wryly.

Rage washed Wellman's face as he turned on Kilarny and Butler. "Get out of here," he yelled. "I don't know what you two were trying to pull, but it'll do you no damned good. Trying to browbeat an old man. I'll see if there's some kind of a charge that will fit what you two did." He stabbed a shaking finger at them. "Just wait. This isn't over with yet. You'll see." His voice grew shriller and shriller. "Now get out of here." He was still screaming "out," as Kilarny closed the door behind him and Butler.

They walked a block before Butler spoke. "Whew. I thought he was going out of his head."

Kilarny chuckled wryly. "Sounded like it, didn't he?"

"Think he'll put some charges against us?" Butler asked.

"I doubt it," Kilarny said. "That would arouse the old question again. Was there or wasn't there a bank robbery at the Wellman Bank?"

"What do you think, Jeff?"

"I think yes," Kilarny said positively. "Did you see Tucker's face? I thought he was going to fall flat in a faint. It's a good thing for Tucker that Wellman came down earlier than usual. It was just rotten timing on our part. I think the old man would have been babbling his guts out by now. Didn't you see how scared he was? Oh, he knows something about that robbery."

"He sure ain't going to talk about it," Butler said glumly.

"Would you," Kilarny asked, "when it was against your boss? Wellman has Tucker thoroughly muzzled."

"You really believe that Rowry came in on the tail end of an actual robbery?"

"I know it."

Butler shook his head. "That ain't going to do Rowry much good. He wanted so much to prove to the town that he wasn't lying."

"I know," Kilarny said. He turned at the next corner to go to his own office. "Tell Rowry I'm sorry it turned out this way. But we've got some knowledge that may help us."

"Damned little," Butler growled.

Kilarny grinned. "Are you thinking that a little knowledge is a dangerous thing?"

"Something like that," Butler replied. He raised a hand in farewell and watched Kilarny stride briskly away. He wondered how things would have turned out if Tucker had been frightened into talking. We'd be a lot better off than we are now, he thought moodily. Poor Rowry. He was going to be so damned disappointed. Well, he'd had disappointments before. He'd just have to learn to live with them.

He walked into his office and had barely gotten settled when Rowry came in. Rowry's eyes were alight with anticipation, and Butler hated to dim that light.

"How did it go, Creed?" Rowry asked eagerly.

"Rotten," Butler said savagely.

"Charley didn't know anything about it?"

"Oh, he knew something about it. It was written all over him. I thought he was going to faint. Then he got enough strength to yell for Wellman. Wellman came out of his office and stopped all our attempts to get information out of Charley."

"What do you think now, Creed?"

"About what?"

"About there being an actual robbery."

"Hell, I believed that from the start. Wellman's protecting that cub of his. But how are we going to bring it to light?"

Rowry sat in a deep study. Somehow the robbery had to be made public information, or else he'd spend the rest of his life in Hays seeing contempt in people's eyes. Oh, it would be there. The trial had seen to that. Even in the short time since the trial, Rowry had seen it in the way people's eyes had avoided him. Some of those people looked as if they wanted to spit on him. He sure wasn't going to take that for very long.

He was so absorbed in his thoughts he didn't see or hear Mayor Reaves come in. Butler's "Good morning, Mayor. What can we do for you?" got Rowry's attention. Reaves stood there, his face red. He wouldn't look at Rowry.

"Marshal, I'm surprised you'd still have a known criminal on your payroll."

Butler bristled immediately. "What the hell is that supposed to mean?"

"It means that the city council and I don't approve of keeping Rowry working for Hays."

"He's no criminal, and you know it," Butler snapped. "I couldn't want a better man. Not a damned thing was proven at that trial. If he goes, you better figure on me going—"

Rowry's shaking head was barely in time to stop the remainder of Butler's words. Butler had been on the verge of quitting. If that happened, there would be nobody left in the office who believed in him.

"You better put it in plain words," Butler growled.

"I want Rowry removed from his position. Immediately! The town and its people will be better off. I know—"

"Will you shut up?" Butler yelled, goaded beyond the limits of his endurance. "I never did think you were too smart. What's happening now only proves it." His voice rose a degree higher. "Will you get out, or do you want me to throw you out?"

Reaves threw him an indignant glance, then turned on his heel and left.

For a long moment, Butler was so angry he couldn't speak. "He's an example of what I don't like in politicians, Rowry. But once they get in power, how are you going to beat them? He's thought it over and decided it'd be smarter if he backed Wellman. I tried, Rowry," he said.

Rowry managed a steady grin. "You sure did. Almost to the point of losing your own job. I knew this was coming, Creed. In fact, when I saw Abby last night, I told her to expect something like this." While he talked, he was unpinning his badge. He laid it on the desk. "Maybe it's turned out for the best. Until I can prove that Wellman is a damned liar, I'll never know any peace in this town."

Butler looked sadly at the badge. When he raised his eyes to Rowry, he asked, "What do you plan on doing, Rowry?"

"Go after Verl, Dent and Chad. When I drag them back and Wellman looks at them, he'll cave in."

"You're looking for a needle in a haystack," Butler warned. "You haven't got the slightest idea where they are."

Rowry nodded in agreement. "I know. But all three are Kansas boys. I doubt if they've gone far beyond Kansas."

"Kansas is big enough."

"I know it," Rowry said, his face grim. "I'll pick out the biggest, the best-known towns." He shrugged. "If I don't find them, I won't be any worse off, will I?"

"I guess not," Butler said morosely. A thought occurred to him, and he asked, "How you fixed for money, Rowry?"

Rowry grimaced. "I could be better off. When I run out, I'll go to work at anything I can find. I'll make it."

There was no use arguing with him. Butler was familiar with that streak of determination. He reached into his pocket and pulled out all the money he had with him. He laid it in front of Rowry and said, "Sorry it isn't more. But that taps me. I'll get by until next payday."

"I'm not taking that," Rowry protested.

"You are," Butler said steadily. "It might give you a little more time to look around. Damn it, this is partly my fight, too. You aren't going to cut me out, are you?"

Rowry looked at those gray eyes. He had seen them when they were cold and steely. Now they were soft and begging. He reached out and picked up the money. "I'm not cutting you out, Creed. Where would you suggest I start?"

Butler's face was all screwed up with his effort to concentrate. "Hays was a dull city for those three hotbloods. After living all their lives here, I'd say they would go for a bigger town, one where they could find some excitement. Damn it, there's so many places to look. As a start, I'd suggest trying Wichita, Abilene, then Dodge City. It'll be a long shot at best," he warned.

Rowry grinned. "I know it, Creed. It'll take time. I've got plenty of that." He wasn't that well-fixed for money. "One thing could help —if I had a picture of them. Do you suppose there's one in town that you could get without arousing a lot of questions?"

Butler gave that some thought, then his face brightened. "Kaffman is the only professional photographer in town. He might have one. I'll check with him, Rowry. Be back as soon as I can."

"I told you I've got all the time in the world."

Butler was gone the better part of an hour. His face was triumphant when he returned. "I got it, Rowry," he crowed. "Maybe this is a good omen." He handed the photograph to Rowry. "Kaffman had to do some digging to find it. He thought he remembered having taken it. He keeps a good file of his past work. It's all of them," he said. "Kaffman didn't have any single pictures. You know the egotistical streak in kids. It's a rare kid who doesn't want a picture of himself. Will it help?"

Rowry studied the picture. All of them were grinning for the camera. Ord was there, and for an instant, Rowry's eyes clouded. He wouldn't have to look for Ord. He would have preferred to have individual pictures, but beggars couldn't be choosers. "I think it's going to be a big help, Creed. I've got to go home and pack a few things. One big advantage of this situation, I don't have to ask you for time off, do I?" He stood and shook hands with Creed.

Butler wrung his hand hard. "I wish it still was the other way around, Rowry. Good luck."

Rowry's teeth flashed. "I'm going to need all I can get." He turned at the door to wave good-bye to Butler.

CHAPTER 20

Doubt assailed Rowry the moment he stepped down from the stage in Wichita. He had never seen anything this big, and he was awed. How was he going to find three people among the throng that packed these streets, even if they were here? He groaned silently at the magnitude of the task.

Well, he couldn't stand around here gawking and get anything done. It was a good thing he had an acquaintance in this city. For two years, he and Scotty Thomas had been close, and Rowry remembered his disappointment when Scotty announced that his family was moving to Wichita. At the age of twelve, such a parting was heartbreaking, and he and Scotty had resolved never to lose touch. Such resolutions were meaningful at that age, but it didn't take much time to weaken them. They had written to each other for four or five months; then that, too, had faded. The last letter Rowry remembered receiving from Scotty had contained the fervent plea, "If you're ever near Wichita, I want you to look me up."

Now Rowry was here to do just that. Scotty was a grown man now, probably married and with his own family. Rowry wondered if the passage of time had changed Scotty much. He sighed in regret at the loss of something that once had been so precious to him. He didn't even have Scotty's address. He would have to ask and see if he could locate him.

He hit pay dirt on his first request. "Scotty Thomas? Sure I know him. Best blacksmith this town's ever had. You want his place of business or his house?"

It was midday, and Rowry said, "His place of business, I guess."

"Go straight down this street about half a mile and you'll see Scotty's building. He's growing. Keeps adding to his place all the time."

Rowry thanked him, picked up his small valise with its rifle strapped to it, and started walking. He could have guessed that Scotty would be a success at whatever he turned to. Even as a school kid, Scotty had a tremendous drive and a knack for working with his hands.

He was hot and dusty when he stopped in front of a big metal building on the southwest corner. He hoped he had made the specified distance. Now the big sign across the building left no doubts. It read SCOTTY THOMAS, BUILDER.

Rowry frowned. The man he had asked directions of had said Scotty was a blacksmith. This sign read differently, but the name was the same.

He went in, and his eyes widened at the bustling activity going on inside the building. He asked for Scotty Thomas, and the man said, "The boss. He's in that office straight ahead of you."

Rowry started to knock, then thought, The hell with it. I know Scotty well enough that I don't have to do that. He opened the door and stepped inside. A half-dozen faces lifted at his entrance, and he didn't think any of them were Scotty. He asked again for Scotty, and the young man at the outer desk said, "He's in that office in the rear." He grinned at Rowry's apparent confusion. "This is the outer office."

Rowry nodded and walked to the small office the man had indicated. He opened the door without knocking; for a moment, the man didn't look up from his work.

That was Scotty, Rowry was positive of it. He had the same unruly tangle of sandy hair and the same broad face. But the face looked so much older. It should, Rowry told himself. Many years had passed. This man was massive, particularly through the chest and shoulders. Maybe he had once been a blacksmith; the development in the chest and shoulders said so.

"Scotty," Rowry said tentatively.

The man raised his head, his momentary annoyance at being interrupted fading. He stared unbelievingly at Rowry and exclaimed, "I'll be goddamned. Rowry?"

"The same." Rowry's chuckle carried his relief. "I got around to coming here a little late."

Scotty stood and bounded toward Rowry. "Rowry," he said. "I didn't think you'd ever get around to coming to see me." His massive arms wrapped around Rowry, and there was strength in that hug. He held Rowry at arm's length and cocked his head to one side. "You've changed. But I would have known you."

"You've changed some, too," Rowry said gravely.

Scotty's deep, booming laugh rang out. "I guess beating on an anvil developed me."

"The man I asked where I could find you told me that you were the best blacksmith in Wichita."

"I hope I was," Scotty said, pride apparent in his voice. "But I gave that up about three months ago. I did real well at blacksmithing, enough to go into something else. I'm building houses now. It's the coming thing in Wichita. Wichita's booming. It grows so much each month that a man hardly recognizes it." He looked shrewdly at Rowry. "Ever think about changing what you're doing?"

Rowry might be looking at a temptation, but he shook his head. It could be a good thing, though. He'd be working for an old friend, apparently one who was doing well. He didn't even have a job in Hays. He had nothing there. He reconsidered that, then shook his head. He had Abby waiting for him.

"No thanks, Scotty. I came up here to find three men." He related all the events that had put him in this mess, and Scotty listened attentively. "I know those three were involved in that robbery," he said. "I want to find them and take them back to Hays. That would tear down a mountain of lies." He pulled the picture out of his pocket and handed it to Scotty. "These are the three I'm looking for."

Scotty studied the picture, then shook his head. "I don't know any of them."

"I didn't expect you to," Rowry replied. "But I thought you might know the marshal of Wichita. Maybe you'd put in a good word for me."

"I know Brad Cummings well," Scotty said. "We're good friends. He'll help you. How about going to see him now?"

"I'm taking you away from your business," Rowry objected.

Scotty winked at him. "That's the advantage of running your own business. You can set your own hours."

They went out a rear door, and Scotty had a buggy waiting there. "You're really living in style," Rowry remarked as he settled himself in the buggy.

Scotty's booming laugh rang out. "Had to have it, Rowry, to get around over town." His face sobered. "I've climbed a high mountain, but it's just as steep coming down and a hell of a lot slipperier. Sometimes when the bills come in at the first of a month, it scares the hell out of me."

"You'll make out," Rowry said. "I know you will."

Scotty must have driven a good two miles before he pulled up in front of a building downtown. My God, just watching the activity going on in this town dizzied Rowry. It was like stepping on an anthill with the ants boiling out. No, he thought, he wouldn't like to live here.

They got down from the buggy and Scotty tied the team to a hitchrack. They walked inside. Scotty greeted a chunky man at a desk. "Brad, how are you doing? I want you to meet an old friend, Rowry Saxton. He's from Hays."

Cummings looked at Rowry as they shook hands. "You're a lawman, aren't you?" he said suddenly.

"Does it show that much?" Rowry asked.

"It does," Cummings said, grinning broadly. "And I'd guess you've been in it for quite a few years. I don't know, but after some years in the business, it puts a stamp on a man you can't miss. What can I do for you, Rowry?"

"I was a lawman," Rowry said. "But I'm not carrying a badge now. Maybe you didn't read about the trial we just had in Hays."

Cummings snapped his fingers. "I did read about the trial, but the name slipped my mind. You're the Saxton named in that trial?"

"The same," Rowry said somberly.

"I didn't read the ending," Cummings said. "How did it turn out?"

"The charges were dismissed when the jury couldn't agree whether or not I was lying about the bank robbery."

"They were stupid," Cummings said brusquely. "If a man does his job well enough to carry a badge several years, you can bet he's no liar. You're after something."

Rowry nodded. He pulled the picture out of his pocket. It was beginning to get dog-eared after all this carrying around. "This one was my brother, the one I shot. The other three got away. The charges being dismissed really didn't clear me. A banker swore his bank wasn't robbed—to protect his son. Like the jury, half the town thinks I'm lying to cover up my real reason for shooting Ord." His face darkened. "The mayor fired me. Goddamn it, I know what I saw," he said fiercely. "I just didn't recognize Ord until it was over."

"Say, you're not on trial here," Cummings said. "So these three are the ones who got away."

"That's them, Brad. Have you seen them?"

Cummings shook his head. "I haven't, and if any of my force have, they haven't mentioned it. Usually they comment on new arrivals in town. But that doesn't really mean anything. People change in this town so fast you can't keep up with them. New arrivals come in daily. Can I keep this picture awhile? I want to show it to my men."

"You can have it until I'm convinced they're not here," Rowry said. "If I have to move on, I'll need it."

"Give yourself a few days," Cummings advised. "If we don't spot them in that time, it's a strong bet that they never came here or are gone. How about starting to look for them after supper? Part of this town doesn't come alive until then."

Rowry stuck out his hand. "I'll be back."

He talked about it to Scotty after they got in the buggy. "I'll give it a week, Scotty. If I can't spot them by that time, it'll be a strong indication they never came here."

"If they're here, Brad will find them," Scotty commented. "He's a good man. Where are you going to stay?"

Rowry grinned sheepishly. "I haven't even thought about that."

"Then you're staying with me."

"I wouldn't want to interrupt your family life," Rowry objected.

"I haven't got any family life," Scotty replied. "At least, not now. That may come later, but first I want to get my business established. You got any other reasons to fuss about?"

Rowry hadn't, and he shook his head. He grabbed at the opportunity to save the drain on his meager resources. Even a cheap room at the lowest rate amounted to a considerable sum by the end of the week. He would still have to face the cost of meals, but with close control he could handle that.

He was back at Cummings' office a little before seven. "You eat?" Cummings asked. He had a toothpick between his teeth. At Rowry's nod, he said, "Good. I just got back. We might as well start out now." As they walked along, Cummings said, "I keep a force of five men. Two for daytime, three for night. I talked to them. None of them has seen your three. But they'll keep an eye out for them, and they know the best places to look."

Rowry couldn't help but feel a surge of hope. With all this help, if the three were here, they would be found. If they're here.

"You're seeing the sleazy part of Wichita," Cummings said. "It's cheaper than the respectable parts of the town. Any bum or crook's more likely to hole up here. Let me do the talking."

Rowry nodded. It would be a big relief to have a man at his side who knew the city.

They stopped in at saloons, brothels and run-down hotels. At each place, Cummings showed the picture Rowry had brought and said a few words. Each time he was answered with negative shakes of heads. He seemed to know all of them, and Rowry remarked on that.

Cummings grinned. "It's just a matter of habit. You see people so many times, and you get to know them. Then I've had to arrest some of them. It all ties up into a neat package. I told all of them I'd appreciate if they heard any word of these three to let me know. Living like they do develops a sharp eye. Even if they only suspect they've spotted the right people, they'll let me know."

It was well after one o'clock when Cummings asked, "Tired?"

"Some," Rowry admitted. "We've kept at it pretty steady."

"I know my legs are damned tired," Cummings said. "Maybe tomorrow night we'll be luckier."

"I hope so," Rowry replied.

Cummings nodded. "Wichita's a fair-sized town. We haven't begun to cover it yet."

Rowry made the long walk to the four-room house Scotty owned. He let himself in with the key Scotty had given him and heard the steady rumbling of Scotty's snoring.

In the morning, Scotty listened to Rowry relating the night's events. "Don't judge Wichita by the part you've seen," he warned. "Brad must've took you through the worst part."

Rowry grinned. "He said something about that. He thinks if the people I'm looking for are here, the poorer part of town would be where they are. I sure saw a lot of women last night," he said reflectively.

"Are you interested in any of them?" Scotty asked, a twinkle in his eyes.

Rowry thought of Abby and shook his head.

"You're just as well off," Scotty said dryly.

"I was just wondering where all those women came from," Rowry said.

Scotty grimaced. "A lot of them are farm girls hankering to get to the big city. Their money runs out—" He shrugged and didn't finish.

"I'm sorry for them," Rowry said and meant it.

"Going out again tonight?"

Rowry nodded. "Brad said we hadn't begun to cover all the bad portion of Wichita." He sighed as he thought of another long evening of walking. One thing was in his favor. He didn't have to report to Cummings until seven o'clock.

"How are you feeling?" Cummings greeted him as he came in. "Ready for some more walking?"

"I'm not looking forward to it, Brad."

"That's the worst part of this job," Cummings said. "All the damned walking. The legs go first. Maybe that's why you don't see any really old law officers. Their legs just gave out on them. Well, let's get at it."

Rowry noticed that Cummings concentrated on the brothels, for most of the night he saw him talking to women. He commented on that, and Cummings grinned. "It just figures. Young bucks like those three are. The first place they'd head for away from home would be a whorehouse."

Rowry thought of all the men the women of the street would entertain, and he asked doubtfully, "Would these women remember them?"

"You can bet on it," Cummings said decisively. "These gals are pretty sharp. They'd remember a new young buck, particularly if his pockets were loaded."

At the end of the night, he shook his head. "Again no luck. Getting discouraged?"

"I knew it'd be a long shot when I picked Wichita. Those three might not even have come here."

"That's right," Cummings agreed. "Well, a couple of more nights should cover the most likely places. The hardest thing to accept is that they might slip into the part we covered yesterday or a couple of days ago." He grimaced. "That's the luck of the game."

Rowry spent two more nights with Cummings, and Cummings said sorrowfully, "I was afraid this could happen, Rowry. You moving on?"

"I'm leaving for Abilene in the morning."

"Say! I might be able to help a little there. Travis Unger, the marshal, is a good friend of mine. In fact, he used to work for me. I'll write a note to him. It could make it easier for you."

"I'd appreciate that, Brad."

He waited until Cummings penned a short note, then tucked it into his pocket. Cummings gave him back his picture, and Rowry put it with the introductory note. He shook hands with Cummings. "I surely appreciate everything you did for me."

"Nothing to thank me for. We'll keep an eye out, and if those three do show up here, I'll get word to you somehow."

Rowry nodded and left the office. The failure of their hunt wasn't Cummings' fault. He had done everything a man could do.

In the morning, he said his farewell to Scotty, and Scotty said, "I still wish you'd consider staying here. I could make it attractive."

Rowry shook his head. "Appreciate it, Scotty. But this is something I've got to do."

"You haven't changed," Scotty said reflectively. "Once you took hold of something, you never let go." He pulled up before the stage depot and said, "I wish you all the luck in the world, Rowry."

If his first stop was any reflection of how his mission would be, Rowry was going to need all that luck. He watched Scotty's buggy diminish in the distance, and there was a lump in his throat. They had promised they would see each other again, but Rowry knew it was doubtful. Each had his own road to travel, and those roads would probably never cross again. He felt strangely lonesome.

CHAPTER 21

Travis Unger was a leaner, younger man than Cummings, but the same stamp was on him. It was in those cold blue eyes and in the cut of his chin.

Rowry had walked in, introduced himself, then pulled out Cummings' note. He saw warmth steal into those blue eyes, softening them. Unger looked up and smiled. "Good old Brad. How's he doing?"

"Complaining about his legs," Rowry said and grinned.

Unger nodded. "The universal complaint of a lawman. What can I do for you?"

He let Rowry talk for an uninterrupted five or six minutes, then looked at the picture Rowry handed him. "I sure haven't seen them," he said regretfully. "But I'll keep an eye out for them. It's their kind that cause a lawman the most trouble. Young and full of piss and vinegar. Where are you staying?"

"At the Drovers' Cottage," Rowry replied. The expenses had nibbled on him while he was in Wichita. It would be worse here, for he would have to pay for his lodging. Each morning he counted his money, and the way it was dwindling was alarming.

"Wish I could give you more time," Unger said. "But two trail herds hit the town at the same time. The town's full of rowdy,

drunken cowboys looking for trouble. By keeping on top of them, I may be able to hold it down."

"Sure, I know." Rowry thought wistfully of working for wages again and even thought of asking for a job. He let that idea slide away from him. That would really tie him up. "If it's all right with you, I'll just wander around town with my eyes open. I may spot them. Is it all right if I carry my rifle with me? I got in the habit of carrying a rifle instead of a pistol."

Unger looked dubious for a moment, then said, "That'll be all right. You might need it if you see them. But don't use it in town for any other reason. Strict regulations here."

Rowry nodded his understanding and walked out. This wasn't going to be a guided tour as it had been in Wichita. Rowry regretted that, but he understood that Unger was in a bind from the rush of events.

He wandered about town, easily spotting the Texans who had driven the trail herds here. They moved with a swinging arrogance to their walk and a belligerence shining brightly from their eyes. Several times he thought that a bunch of them would stop and hurrah him, but his steady eyes and purposeful look must have deterred them. He passed the famous stock pens across from the Drovers' Cottage, the pens stretching more than a mile. One of the herds was being loaded into the long string of cattle cars pulled up beside the pens. The lamentations of the cattle and the profanity of the cowboys filled the air as the cowboys tried to hurry the cattle up the ramps and into the cars.

It was always a show, and quite a crowd had gathered to watch it. Rowry peered at each face, the familiar disappointment returning after each look.

He passed the famous Bull Head Saloon, stopping for a moment to stare at the sign that had brought it such notoriety. It was a painting of a bull in all its masculine glory. The womenfolk had complained about the vulgarity of such naturalism. The Hays paper had run an account about the famous saloon, and Rowry had read every word. The women had complained so vigorously that the owner of the saloon had tried to have the objectionable parts of the animal painted out. It hadn't been successful, for the original painting had

shown through. It didn't take much close observation to see what the original painting had looked like. Rowry shook his head. He thought the whole argument was a piece of damned foolishness. The women of Abilene saw dozens of bulls in the streets every day. They knew what a bull looked like. He imagined that some prudish old woman had started the fight and had gathered support to her righteous cause. It was a lesson to the males; never buck a determined bunch of women. He started to move on, then on impulse decided to go into the saloon. He would never be any closer; he might as well go inside and see the saloon firsthand. Even his dwindling resources would allow him a beer.

The place was crammed, and the incessant babble of talk was almost deafening. The bar was lined solidly, elbow to elbow, broken every now and then by a saloon girl in her gaudy dress.

One girl collared him before he had gone five paces into the place. She ran a hand under his arm and said in a wheedling voice, "Want to buy a girl a drink, mister?"

There was no real regret in Rowry's shaking head. The paint on her face didn't cover all the age lines and weariness etched there. "I've only got enough to afford a beer," he said, smiling into those eager eyes. That doused her ardor as effectively as if he had dashed a bucket of cold water on her. She disengaged her hand and strode away.

Rowry made the beer last a full fifteen minutes until the bartender's unfriendly eyes shouted a message that wasn't hard to read. Buy up or move out.

Rowry grinned into those unfriendly eyes. "Just leaving," he murmured. That brief respite had given him a chance to make a hurried survey of the men lining the bar. Most of the faces he studied in the reflections in the backbar mirror. The faces were all young, filled with rowdy life, but none of them were of the men he wanted.

On the way out, Rowry passed the woman who had tried to wheedle a drink out of him. He touched the brim of his hat to her, and she sniffed at him. He was glad he wasn't close enough for her to spit at him.

He spent three more days in Abilene, covering as much of the town as he could. At the end of those three days, he was sick with

disappointment. He felt pretty certain that if those three had been here, they had moved on. His accommodations at the Drovers' Cottage were costing him dearly, even though he had asked for the cheapest room. The price of meals was another staggering blow. He was damned glad he didn't live here permanently. The few dollars remaining in his pockets made his decision for him. After paying his fare to Dodge City, he would have damned little left.

He stopped by to tell Unger of his decision, and Unger said, "No luck, huh?"

"I didn't see them," Rowry answered.

"I wish I could have been of more help," Unger said and meant it. "A couple of nights ago, a bunch of drunken cowboys decided to buffalo the town. Kept me up all night. By the time I got the ruckus quieted down and had them locked up, there wasn't much left in me. God, why does a man ever decide to carry a badge?"

"I guess some instinct in him pushes him," Rowry replied.

"As good an answer as any," Unger said gloomily. "Good luck to you."

"It looks like I'm going to need it," Rowry answered soberly. He walked out and turned in the direction of the stage depot.

CHAPTER 22

After paying for his ticket to Dodge City, Rowry had three dollars and some small change in his pocket. That wouldn't pay for much more than one day's expenses, and bitter experience told him that would hardly get him started on his search. The moment he landed in Dodge City, he had to do something about his resources.

The stage pulled up at the depot in Dodge City, and Rowry descended from it, wincing a little as his cramped and aching muscles protested at his activity.

Dodge City was the last arrow in his quiver. Of course, there were many more cities and towns in Kansas, but he had no guarantee that the three had gone to any of them. Worse, he didn't have the money to explore any of those towns. The first thing he had to do was find a job, any kind of job as long as it paid him enough to live on.

He had never been in Dodge City before. He walked down Front Street, his eyes alight with interest. He read the big sign on the saloon across the street. He supposed the Long Branch Saloon had gotten more publicity than any other saloon. He might as well start looking for a job there.

At this time of day, the place wasn't busy. Two bartenders lolled behind the bar, waiting for the inevitable rush that would come later. It was a damned big place, and Rowry speculatively eyed the huge floor space. It would take a lot of broom strokes.

He walked up to the bar and asked the nearest bartender, "Can I talk to the boss?"

The man eyed him with practiced indifference. "What for?"

Rowry didn't resent his nosiness. Perhaps that was on the boss's orders. "I'd like to see him about a job."

The bartender's interest quickened, and Rowry thought there might be some hostility in it. "You a bartender?"

Rowry quickly shook his head. "I don't have that kind of skill," he said.

It was a mild form of flattery, and Rowry thought it might have softened the bartender. "I want to ask him for the swamping job. Swinging a broom doesn't take much skill."

"Cash is in the back office. Through that door." A jerk of his thumb indicated the office. "You might be in luck. Cash kicked old George's butt out of here last night. George showed up drunk one too many times."

"What's his last name?" Rowry asked. At the bartender's perplexed frown, he said, "I mean Cash's."

The bartender grinned. "I thought you were asking about George. Cash Delaney. He's a square shooter. Treat him right, and he'll treat you the same way."

"Thanks," Rowry murmured and walked toward the door. His belly was tight. He needed this job bad. He rapped on the door.

"Come in," a heavy voice called.

Rowry opened the door and started toward the desk at the end of the room. It was the biggest office he had ever seen, and his uncertainty rose with each step. A huge man sat behind the desk, and those black eyes in a broad, florid face never left Rowry. "Yes?" he said in an unfriendly voice.

Rowry gulped, then got his jumping pulse under control. All this man could do was turn him down. "Mr. Delaney," he said, and his voice was steady. "I'm looking for a job. Any kind, as long as it pays enough for me to live on." He started to say he knew about old George being kicked out, then held it. Maybe Delaney wouldn't appreciate his employees bandying about intimate news.

The dark eyes weighed him thoroughly. "You particular?"

Rowry shook his head. "No, sir. Any kind of honest work."

"I fired the swamper I had last night," Delaney said with brutal directness. "He showed up drunk once too often." Those eyes ran over Rowry again. "You a drinking man?"

"No, sir. Mainly because I never could afford it, I guess."

Delaney's heavy features relaxed. "Good. The pay is two dollars a day. You can sleep in the storeroom. Take it or leave it."

Rowry almost sighed in relief. It wasn't a princely wage, but with his lodging thrown in, he could make it. Of course, working at a regular job would cut his looking time down, but he would be on the scene. "Thanks, Mr. Dela—" he started.

Delaney went back to his figures. "Don't thank me now. You ain't got anything yet. Do a bad job, and I'll kick your butt out as fast as I did old George's."

"You won't have any reason to kick me out," Rowry said.

Delaney's grunt was his only response. Rowry turned and walked that interminable distance to the door.

He closed it behind him, and both bartenders were watching him. "Did you get it?" the one who had talked to Rowry asked.

Rowry nodded. "I did." The less he said on a new job, the better off he'd be.

"I told Jack you would. You had Cash in a kind of a bind. He may look like a hard-nosed man, but he's a generous man underneath. Do the right thing for him, and he'll reward you." He squinted curiously at Rowry. "You don't look like the ordinary swamper."

"I'm not," Rowry said quietly. "A streak of bad luck—" He shrugged and let it go at that.

"You don't look like a gambling man, either," the bartender commented.

Rowry's startled frown disappeared as he understood why the bartender said that. That "streak of bad luck" had turned him in the wrong direction. Rowry let it go without explanation. "Where can I find brooms and mops?" he asked.

"In the storeroom," the bartender answered. "This way." He led Rowry to a big room on the other side of Delaney's office. The room was crammed with everything, mostly cases of liquor. It was a messy room. Rowry intended to straighten it out the moment he found the time. He took off his jacket and left his valise and rifle in an empty corner.

"Good thing you're getting rid of that rifle," the bartender said seriously. "Bat doesn't like guns carried openly in town, particularly handguns."

"I don't own a handgun," Rowry said.

Curiosity remained in the bartender's eyes. There was something about this man that bothered him. He certainly wasn't the run-of-the-mill swamper. "Just ask if there's something you want that you can't find."

"I'll do that," Rowry replied. "Thanks for everything."

The bartender shook his head and left. A mannerly cuss and not like the broom pushers he had known. For some reason, he was down on his luck. The bartender speculated on that, then let it go. It was none of his business.

Rowry looked around the storage room before he started to work. This was a far cry from luxury, but it was shelter. He would survive.

He decided to sweep the floor first. He had noticed upon entering the Long Branch that the floor wasn't very clean. It had evidently rained in Dodge recently, for tracks of mud were ground into the floor. Old George hadn't been the most meticulous of swampers.

He found a broom and approved of it. Its bristles were in good shape, and it wouldn't leave streaks of debris. At least Delaney furnished suitable tools.

He thought about Bat as he worked. That had to be Bat Masterson. Masterson had been a deputy marshal when he had met him. Evidently, Masterson had climbed a notch since then. It had been four years ago that Rowry first knew him. Masterson had come to Hays in the fall, looking for a little bird hunting. He had stopped in at Creed's office to ask information, and Creed said, "Ask Rowry here. He's a bird hunter. And he knows the country. Better still, Rowry, go with him. You could stand some bird hunting, couldn't you? It's been a long stretch since you've had any time off."

Rowry had changed his rifle for a shotgun from the gun rack. Masterson had commented upon Butler's generosity with time off. "Sounds like you've got a good boss."

"The best, Bat. We won't need horses. A short walk, and you'll be in open country."

"You're the boss," Masterson said. He was a likable man, handsome in a rough-hewn manner, with a mustache standing out sharply against his pale features. Rowry kept staring curiously at Masterson's hat. He had never seen one like it before.

Masterson finally noticed it and grinned. "Haven't you ever seen a derby? They call it a bowler in England. It's high style over there."

"Maybe," Rowry conceded. But this was America. Damned if he'd ever wear such a ridiculous piece of headgear.

They had had a successful day, Rowry topping Masterson's bag. "You're good with that scatter-gun," Masterson said. "But a handgun is my game."

"Mine's a rifle," Rowry replied. They had engaged in an argument about the respective values of handguns and rifles. "A handgun's faster," Masterson said.

"Not that much," Rowry had objected. "I can get a rifle in play fast enough. A rifle's got more shock impact, and it reaches out farther. I'll stick to my rifle."

"It's not accurate if you have to use it in a hurry," was Masterson's final objection.

"Maybe I can prove it tomorrow," Rowry said. During the hunt, Masterson had decided to stay over another day.

"That's something I'll have to see," Masterson said cynically.

Rowry had taken his rifle with him. Depositing his shotgun against a tree, he had moved out, walking stealthily. What he had in mind would take difficult shooting, but he had made some positive statements yesterday. He either made good on them, or he looked like a braggart.

His eyes inspected the terrain before him. He saw the flutter of motion in a covey ahead of them. They were ready to break. "Hold it," he said softly, checking Masterson. He flicked up the rifle barrel and squeezed off a shot. He hit the cock quail squarely in the head, and it dropped with only a flutter. The rest of the flock flew away.

"I wouldn't have believed it," Masterson said, "if I hadn't been here and seen it." He picked up the cock's body and stared at it. The head was missing. "One hell of a shot, Rowry. But I can duplicate it with a handgun."

At the skepticism in Rowry's eyes, he said, "I guess it's up to me to prove it."

It took another half hour of hunting before Masterson could spot the covey he wanted. He motioned with his hand for Rowry to be quiet. He wore a holstered gun, and his hand flashed to the butt of the gun. It came up in one fast, blurred motion, then the gun roared. The bullet hit the hen quail squarely.

"I'll be damned," Rowry said, amazed. He walked over and picked up the mangled body. The heavy .45 slug had virtually wrecked the little body.

"I left the best meat," he said and grinned.

Masterson had roared with delight over that. "You topped me there," he admitted. "I'm just as happy that we won't have to face each other."

"Agreed, Bat."

Rowry smiled unconsciously as he plied the broom. That incident had sealed a friendship. Masterson had promised he would come back, and Rowry had vowed he would come to Dodge City. He hadn't until now. Oh, he could have gone straight to Bat, stated his dilemma, and Masterson would have offered him enough help to tide him over. Rowry had too much pride to do that.

He finished sweeping the floor, and he had a sizable pile of sweepings near the front door. "All right to sweep it out the door?"

"That's what old George did with it," the bartender answered. "But he never got it so clean."

Rowry nodded. A few flicks of the broom, and the sweepings flew out of the door.

He went back to the storeroom and got a mop and a pail. He filled the pail with soapy water.

He plied the mop with long strokes, and the bartender said, "Jesus Christ, Jack. Would you look at that? Hey, who are you trying to impress?"

"Cash," Rowry said. "I just want to be sure he won't fire me."

"He won't," the bartender said. "Not after he sees this floor."

Rowry dumped the dirty water outside and headed for the storeroom. "Going to knock off for a nap?" the bartender called.

Rowry shook his head. "Got something else to do. If anybody wants me, I'll be in the storeroom."

Delaney found him busy arranging the storeroom. He had better than half of it done, rearranging the liquor cases and stacking them higher than his head.

Delaney stared at what Rowry had accomplished, and his jaw sagged. "Who told you to do this?" he demanded.

"Nobody, sir. But it was so damned messy." He grinned. "I hardly had room to stretch out."

"My God, I don't believe it," Delaney said. "I just saw your floor. It's clean enough to eat off it. If you keep up this kind of work, I've hired me a treasure."

"I'll keep it up."

Delaney turned to leave, then came back. "I offered you two dollars a day, didn't I?"

Rowry nodded.

"Well, beginning immediately, it's three dollars. Nobody can say Cash Delaney cheats a man. At least you can buy yourself a decent meal tonight." He counted off three ones into Rowry's palm, then, on a generous impulse, added another dollar. "Buy yourself the best meal you can find."

The grin hadn't faded from Rowry's face when the door closed. Ever since he was a kid he had practiced the principles of hard work and self-application. Those principles still worked.

He went out for his evening meal. The bartender had recommended Delmonico's, and Rowry decided to try it. The Long Branch had been filling up when he left it. He had scrutinized every face; he wouldn't allow disappointment to overwhelm him. This was only his first night here. He was earning enough money to last him as long as he wanted the job.

He ordered the most expensive meal on the menu and chewed appreciatively on the steak. He could be grateful to Cash Delaney for this meal. He ate a leisurely meal and came out of the restaurant thoroughly satisfied. He hadn't seen Masterson yet, but he could bet he would. Masterson would keep a close eye on his town.

He looked with distaste at all the dirt the booted feet of the customers lining the bar had brought in. That meant another thorough cleaning job in the morning. He should be grateful to those customers instead of criticizing them. They were the reason he had a job.

If anything, the Long Branch was even fuller now. The bartender beckoned him over and said, "Cash left something for you in the storeroom."

"What is it?"

"You'll see," the man said and grinned. "By the way, Cash also said to let you have anything you want at the bar."

Rowry shook his head. "I'm not a drinking man."

"I'll be goddamned," the bartender said in amazement. "If I had made an offer like that to old George, I'd have been trampled under in the rush."

Rowry smiled at him and walked to the storage room. He could do nothing until morning when the place would be empty. He opened the door and stared for a long moment. A cot was there with a pillow on it and a couple of folded new blankets. Rowry felt his eyes sting. This was proof that his principles worked and kept working. He was going to have a comfortable night.

CHAPTER 23

Rowry was busy cleaning the floor in the morning. He heard some-one come in, but he didn't look around.

"Rowry?" There was a startled note in the voice.

Rowry slowly turned. He knew that voice. Bat Masterson stood there, still wearing that ridiculous hat. He bounded toward Rowry, his hand extended. "I thought it was you, but from the back I couldn't be sure. What the hell are you doing in here, and what's the broom for?"

Rowry wrung Masterson's hand hard. "Just what it looks like. Sweeping the floor."

Masterson scowled at him. "There has to be something behind all this. Come on. I want to hear all about it."

Rowry sighed and leaned his broom against a table. "I got fired in Hays, Bat. I came here needing a job. Cash was good enough to offer me this. I'm doing the best I can to hold it."

Masterson swore fluently. "There's more to the story than that. Come on, give! I want to hear it all."

Rowry briefly related his story from the beginning. "Believe me, I sweat during that trial. But it was a hung jury, and the judge dismissed the case. The only way I could get my standing back was to find those three kids."

Masterson shook his head in disgust. "You must have some stupid people in Hays."

"We've got our share," Rowry said dryly. "I'd still like to be able to go back there and hold my head high. I looked for those three in Wichita and Abilene. Nothing. Just as I landed in Dodge, I ran out of money."

"And you wouldn't come to me," Masterson said accusingly. "I thought we were friends."

"You can still think it," Rowry said firmly. "What I did is proof of it. I didn't know what I might be interrupting or how much of a burden I'd put on you."

The accusation didn't leave Masterson's face. "You didn't consider me a very good friend, did you?"

Rowry sighed. He was going to have to do some talking to make Masterson see all of this in the right light. Before he could explain further, Delaney came in. He saw the two talking, and he came up to them, a worried look on his face.

"Bat, I don't give a damn what he's done. I can vouch for him. He's the most reliable man I ever hired."

Masterson grinned wickedly. "He's not so reliable to me. Cash, I'm afraid I'm going to have to take him in."

"What's he done?" Delaney asked belligerently. "I'm telling you he must have had some kind of reason."

Rowry laughed and said, "Don't pay any attention to him, Cash. That's just Bat's odd sense of humor. He doesn't want me for anything. Tell him, Bat."

"I don't want him, Cash," Masterson said and grinned. "I've known Rowry for years. He's one of the best lawmen I've ever known."

"A lawman?" Delaney's face was shocked. "What's he doing working here in such a lowly job?"

"That was what I was waiting for him to establish," Masterson said. "He was getting into it when you came up. I'm sorry, Cash, but I'm going to have to take him with me."

"You can't do that to me," Delaney wailed. "Just when I think I've got a problem solved, something comes along and knocks it over. Damn it, Bat. You don't know how much trouble I've had keeping a good swamper. You don't have to go, do you, Rowry?"

"I'm afraid I do, Cash," Rowry said regretfully. "I want to tell you how much I appreciate everything you did for me. I'm going to get my rifle and belongings out of the storeroom."

He was gone for only a moment. When he returned, Delaney and Masterson were arguing. "Damn it, Bat, you tell me where I can get a good swamper."

"I'll send over the next drunk I arrest," Masterson said, grinning broadly.

"Oh hell," Delaney said in disgust. "I just fired one of those. I want Rowry."

"You can't have him," Masterson said firmly and took hold of Rowry's arm.

When they got outside, Rowry said, "Poor Cash. I feel sorry for him."

"You don't have to bleed for him so much," Masterson said indifferently. "He'll get along."

Rowry glanced at Masterson's derby. "You're still wearing that silly hat."

"No, this is a new one," Masterson replied. "My old one blew off and sailed right under the rear wheel of a stagecoach. It flattened it, and I couldn't get it poked out again."

"It's too bad you found a new one," Rowry said.

Nettled, Masterson said, "You're still carrying that rifle. On a lawman, it looks as silly as you say my hat does."

Rowry chuckled. "This is a new one. Those punks swung my rifle against a tree trunk. Snapped the stock clean off." He chuckled again. "I guess we're even, Bat."

"Even," Masterson said and smiled.

They walked to Masterson's office, and Rowry sank happily into a chair. This smelled like a lawman's office. It was like going home.

"Leave out anything, Rowry, about your troubles?"

Rowry pulled the now battered picture of the four youths from his pocket. Much more of this hard usage, and he wouldn't be able to show it any longer. "The shortest is Ord. I shot him during the bank robbery. The other three got away."

Masterson studied the picture intently. "They look like young punks."

Rowry nodded. "They are. About twenty years old, Bat. Have you seen them?"

Masterson shook his head. "No, I haven't. But that doesn't mean anything. The way people come and go in this town, you see them one day, and the next they're gone. They could be holed up in one of a dozen hovels. There's a certain element in this town that will gladly harbor a criminal."

Rowry was appalled. "You mean even if they are here, it could take weeks to find them."

"More likely months," Masterson said grimly. "I've known of a couple of wanted men who hid out here in Dodge for almost a year. They got to lusting after a woman and ventured out of hiding. That got them caught." He snapped his fingers and exclaimed, "Say! That gives me an idea. About three weeks ago a new gal showed up to work in one of the houses. You never saw a woman with such a build. She looked like the Venus de Milo come to life. She was the talk of the town in a few days. If she can hold up, she's bound to make a fortune."

"Bat, you sound like you're speaking from firsthand experience."

Masterson flushed. "A good lawman has to keep abreast of what's going on in his town, doesn't he? Get that stupid grin off your face. I only went there once."

"What happened?" Rowry asked in mock seriousness.

"I was struck dumb when I saw her, but one thing ruined everything." He paused a moment, his eyes narrowed in reflection.

"What was that?"

"She never stopped talking. She started the moment she began taking off her clothes and never stopped a second, not even in the most intimate moment." He shook his head in disgust. "Once was enough for me. I couldn't stand her incessant chatter. But she might do you a favor."

Rowry threw up a hasty hand. "Not me." He wasn't looking for that kind of woman, no matter how beautiful she was.

"I wasn't suggesting you go there," Masterson said and guffawed. "But with this talk about her getting all over town, it should reach the men you want. Those young punks couldn't resist a temptation like that, could they?"

Rowry seriously considered the suggestion. Why not? he thought. Those three had money in their pockets, and they were foot free. "It's worth looking into," he said.

Rowry and Masterson were across from the house of ill repute shortly after eight o'clock that evening. "They sure do a hell of a business," Rowry commented after watching a steady stream of customers come and go.

"Makes a man think seriously about going into the business," Masterson said, chuckling. "You'd know those three if you saw them?"

"I'd know them," Rowry said positively.

They remained where they were until after midnight. Masterson stretched and said, "Looks like they're not going to show tonight."

"No," Rowry agreed unhappily. "Even if they are in town."

"You didn't lose anything but a little time," Masterson argued. "It beats trying to dig them out of some rabbit hole. Let's go and get some shut-eye."

Masterson lived in a boarding house, and he shared his room with Rowry. The last thing Rowry said before he fell asleep was, "Bat, I'm going to pay all this back."

"Who's asking for payment of any kind?" Masterson retorted. "Will you shut up and let me get some sleep?"

They spent a second night outside the infamous house. Again Rowry watched the steady stream of customers. None of them were the ones he wanted.

"They're not coming," he said morosely.

"I still think it's a damned good idea," Masterson said. "Because they don't show up for a couple of nights doesn't mean they're never coming. You can't expect a man to be aroused every night."

Rowry groaned. "How long do you think it will take?"

Masterson considered the question. "I'd say at least a week. But with young bucks, it should happen sooner."

"That means we'll be back here again tomorrow night," Rowry said wearily.

"You want them, don't you?" Masterson asked.

They took the same place the third night, under the spreading branches of a gnarled elm tree. This kind of inactivity ground on a man's nerves, and Rowry kept shifting restlessly. Another misspent night, he was just beginning to think, when he stiffened as he stared down the street. "Against the tree, Bat," he hissed. "Don't move. It could be them."

The three moved steadily toward the entrance of the bawdy house. A woman met them there, and they stopped to exchange a few remarks. The light was bright enough to see them plainly.

"It's them," Rowry said simply. He didn't feel any sense of exultation. He just felt weary. "Do we go in after them?" he asked Masterson.

"I'd say wait until they come out," Masterson answered. He grinned at Rowry. "You wouldn't want to spoil their fun, would you? It could be the last they'll know in a long time. Besides, they'll be spent and careless. It'll be easier to take them."

"All three of them were armed," Rowry warned.

Masterson shrugged. "There's two of us to take three punks. The odds aren't strong enough in their favor."

Rowry began to fret after half an hour. "Suppose they're not coming out this way. They could slip out a back door and—"

"Will you quit stewing?" Masterson interrupted him. "You saw how busy the place was tonight. They may have had to do some waiting for the women they wanted. All three could want the same woman. That would take some time, wouldn't it?"

"I guess so," Rowry muttered.

"We oughta move across the street," Masterson suggested. "They'll be coming out any time now."

They crossed the street and took up positions behind a huge lilac bush. It would afford them good shelter.

The minutes dragged on drearily. Rowry knew that better than an hour had passed. He started to express his doubts when Masterson uttered a satisfied "Ah." The ring of triumph was so evident that Rowry didn't try to question him. He parted the foliage of the bush and peered through the opening. The three he wanted were coming out of the house.

They were in good spirits. They horsed around, punching each other and laughing boisterously.

"Let them get down the street a little way," Masterson whispered. "I think we can close in on them without them even being aware of it."

They dropped in behind the three, and their faster pace was steadily cutting down the intervening distance. So far, the kids had no suspicion they were being followed. A faint noise or some instinct must have warned one of them, for he stopped and began to turn his head.

"Hold it right where you are," Masterson snapped. "Or each of you will get a hole through his head. Unbuckle those gun belts and drop them on the ground."

"Is this a holdup?" Verl asked sullenly.

"No, Verl, it isn't. You and Dent and Chad have done all of that that's going to happen." The happiness was setting in, and Rowry was almost giddy with it. "Bat means exactly what he says. Easy," he warned as all three started to turn. "Drop those guns." His voice crackled. "Right now."

All three unbuckled their gun belts, and Rowry heard the guns hit the ground. "You stupid kids," he said, his rage beginning to shake his voice. "You stopped running too soon. You shouldn't have stopped until you got to Mexico."

The three turned and looked at Rowry. "Oh, Jesus," Chad wailed. "It's Rowry."

"Didn't you think I'd catch up with you?" Rowry asked. "I had a lot tied up in you three. You got Ord killed." The vicissitudes of the long search were beginning to set in, and he was starting to tremble. "Move, damn you."

"Where are you taking us?" Verl asked sullenly.

"To a banquet in celebration of your deeds," Rowry snapped.

"Shut up, Rowry," Masterson said quietly.

Rowry nodded. He was talking too much, and Masterson knew it. "You're going to jail," Rowry said. He was in full control again. "Move! You even try to break for it, and you're dead before you know it."

The three looked at the rifle and pistol trained on them and decided they had no chance. They turned and began to move as Masterson directed.

Rowry only hesitated to scoop up the three gun belts. He draped them over an arm and quickened his step to catch up with Masterson.

"You did it, Rowry," Masterson said.

"No, you did it," Rowry corrected. "If it hadn't been for you—"

"You're talking too much again," Masterson warned.

Rowry grinned at him. "I won't say another word until we get them locked up."

"That'll be a relief," Masterson said mockingly.

The three were marched to jail and locked up in a cell after each had been thoroughly searched. Masterson looked at the small pile of wadded-up bills on the desk. "Makes you believe that crime can pay. There's a little over seven thousand there."

"It didn't pay for them," Rowry said and smiled. After all the bleak days of frustration, he didn't believe he could be so happy.

"What are you going to do with them, Rowry?"

The question puzzled Rowry a little. "Why, take them back to Hays." His job wouldn't be done until he had delivered them to the Hays jail.

"That could be difficult," Masterson mused.

Rowry started to protest, and Masterson held up a hand, checking Rowry's outburst. "Let me think. I'm figuring out the best way to get them back." He sat there a moment in silence, then nodded in satisfaction. "Hell, it's simple. We'll hire a stagecoach to be sure no one but them and their guard are on it."

"That's over a hundred miles," Rowry objected. "It'd cost a fortune."

"You want to be positive you get them back, don't you? I've got enough money to pay the charge."

"You can't do that, Bat," Rowry began. "I can't let you—"

"Oh, damn it," Masterson said wearily. "You're sure windy tonight. You can send it back to me."

Rowry nodded and gave in. "I'll never be able to repay you, Bat."

"I'm thinking of dropping by this fall for some more bird hunting. If I remember right, you topped me both days."

"I can't top you in this," Rowry said. Damn, but his eyes were stinging.

"I'm going to send a deputy along with you," Masterson said. He held up a hand again. "Don't start any of that nonsense again. I'm just making sure you get them back." He thought a moment longer. "I'd better make arrangements for a stage to be here about dawn. The fewer people who know about it, the better off you'll be. Go on, grab a few winks. I'll make all the arrangements for the deputy and the stage."

"I'll take the cell next to them," Rowry said. "If they make as much as a sound, I'll be there to come down on them hard."

Masterson sauntered toward the door. "I wouldn't want to be thinking about what's filling those three heads tonight. Be back as soon as I can."

Masterson locked the door behind him, and Rowry took the cell next to the three prisoners. They were whispering among themselves, and Rowry couldn't make out a word. He was suddenly enraged. These three had cost him a lot in worry and sorrow and frustration. "Stop that talking," he roared. "One more sound, and I'd just as soon leave you dead here."

It was an idle threat, though the three didn't know that. They didn't know how vital it was to Rowry to get them back to Hays.

CHAPTER 24

Dawn was only a thin gray band of light in the east when Masterson shook Rowry awake. "Stage is outside, Rowry," he said softly.

Rowry came to with a start. He looked wildly at the cell holding the three prisoners and said, "Damn me for falling asleep."

Masterson shook his head. "No harm done. My deputy and I watched them. Want to get them loaded?"

"I want them handcuffed," Rowry said firmly. "Maybe even leg-irons after we get them in the stage. I'm taking no chances of losing them."

"Don't blame you," Masterson agreed.

The three men were handcuffed before they were marched out to the stage. After they climbed in, Masterson and Rowry put leg-irons on each of them. "You shouldn't have any trouble with them," Masterson commented. "Rowry, this is Frank Garfield, a thoroughly reliable man."

Rowry shook hands with a thin, tough-looking man. "One of you will be able to be awake at all times," Masterson said. He motioned up to the driver. "And this is Lem Marker. One of the best drivers I know."

Marker reached down, and Rowry stretched to meet the extended hand. Marker had watched the proceedings with interest. "Three young whippersnappers," he said and spat out into the street. "I swear the younger generation doesn't get any better. They think they can get away with anything."

"These three won't get away with anything more," Rowry said. "Lem, how long do you figure it'll take you to make Hays?"

Marker closed one eye while he calculated. "Leaving this early, I should be pulling into Hays by nightfall."

"That'll do just fine," Rowry said. He didn't want to be driving through Hays in daylight.

Masterson went into the office and came back with a huge sack. "Sandwiches," he said. "Enough for all of you. You won't eat fancy, but it'll do you." He put the sack on the floor of the stage, then pulled money out of his pocket. He had straightened out the wadded-up bills. "The bank's money," he said. "You wouldn't want to forget that."

"I sure wouldn't," Rowry said gravely. He carefully placed the money in a pants pocket. "I'll feel rich at least until I get to Hays." He shook hands with Masterson. "Bat, I don't know how to thank you."

"Then don't try," Masterson said brusquely. "I'll look forward to seeing you in the fall."

"This time, I'll let you outshoot me," Rowry said and chuckled.

"We'll see about that," Masterson replied.

Rowry climbed into the stage and sat beside Garfield.

"This is going to be a miserable trip," Verl said sullenly. "We're ironed up like wild animals."

"Tough," Rowry said. "You should have thought of that before you started on that spree." He settled back as he heard Marker release the brakes.

"Come on, my beauties," Marker yelled. The words were followed by the sharp cracking of the whip.

The abrupt start pushed Rowry and Garfield farther back into the cushions, then they lurched forward. "Always love a stage trip," Garfield said sourly. "A man is so fresh when he finishes one." He looked at the shackled prisoners. "But I'll bet we'll feel a hell of a lot better than those three."

Rowry laughed. "You know, I couldn't feel any better." He was going home.

Verl kept complaining bitterly about how uncomfortable he was until it got on Rowry's nerves. "Shut up," he snapped. "You got yourself into this mess," he said. "If you're looking for somebody to blame, try yourself."

Verl started to say something, and Rowry said coldly, "Keep your damned mouth closed. I mean it. Or maybe a few licks across your mouth will close it for you."

Verl couldn't meet Rowry's eyes; he looked down at his handcuffed wrists.

Garfield laughed. "He probably should have had that kind of treatment a long time ago. Then maybe he wouldn't be sitting here. I ain't got no sympathy for some of our younguns. They get themselves in a hole too deep to climb out, then howl because nobody's standing near to reach a hand down to them."

Rowry nodded soberly. That was God's truth. He guessed it took some age before a man could see that.

The miles rolled by, and the countryside racing past the stage window had a mesmerizing effect on Rowry. His eyes grew heavier, and his head bobbed until his chin hitting his chest jolted him awake.

"Why don't you go ahead and take a nap?" Garfield suggested. "You look like you need it."

"Think I will," Rowry replied. He settled back in a corner of the seat and said, "Frank, I'm damned glad you're along." He was asleep almost before he finished the words.

He didn't know how long he slept, but he felt refreshed when he opened his eyes. He looked out of the window and asked, "Where are we?"

"We just passed through Kinsley," Garfield replied.

Rowry whistled. The sun wasn't very high. Marker was making excellent time. "Lem said he could make Hays by nightfall," he remarked.

"If anybody can do what he says, Lem can," Garfield said. "I never saw a driver who could get more out of his horses."

Rowry looked over at the prisoners. All three were asleep. Rowry couldn't help feeling some pity for them. They had so much of their lives to live, and they had blighted everything.

Marker pulled the stage to a stop about noon. Rowry thrust an inquiring face out of the window, and Marker said, "Thought I'd give the horses a breather. I figure I'm ahead of schedule."

"How about something to eat?" Rowry suggested. "Bat sent a whole sack of sandwiches along."

"I could use a couple of them," Marker said and cackled. "I brought along some oats for the horses. Might as well feed them while we're here." He climbed down and looked into the stage. "Might be a good chance to let the prisoners stretch their legs."

Rowry's first inclination was to refuse, then he reconsidered. Chained as the prisoners were and with him and Garfield so close by, there was no chance of the three escaping. Where could they go?

Rowry ordered the prisoners out of the stage. With the handcuffs and leg-irons, it was a difficult task climbing to the ground.

"Want some sandwiches?" Rowry offered, holding out the sack.

"You expect us to eat with these on?" Verl held up his manacled wrists.

Rowry shrugged. "Suit yourself. I don't give a damn one way or the other."

Verl and Dent reconsidered, and each took a sandwich. Chad shook his head. "I'm not hungry." He looked frightened.

Rowry looked at him, then shrugged. "It's your decision." He started to move away, then said, "You better take care of all your personal problems. Once we get rolling again, it'll be a long time before we stop."

Verl looked at him with hate-filled eyes. "I wish we'd have gotten you the night we had a crack at you."

Rowry grinned. "I'll bet you do. It looks like you missed a lot of opportunities. You could have stayed straight."

Marker removed the feed bags from the muzzles of the horses and signaled that he was ready. Rowry herded the prisoners back into the stage. "Your turn," he said to Garfield.

"My eyes are getting heavy," Garfield confessed. "Always happens whenever I take a stage trip."

"Go ahead," Rowry said.

He sat there facing the three prisoners. Every time their eyes met full on, he could see the hatred in their eyes. Stupid kids, he thought. It was a form of sympathy. They thought they had every reason to hate him. That hatred should be directed at themselves.

Marker had swung north after Kinsley, and he had a straight run to Hays. He stopped again at Rush Center, and he was pleased with himself. "Ain't those beauties something?" he asked, meaning the horses. "I'm making better time than I thought I would. Hell, I could make it into Hays about sundown."

Rowry shook his head. "Slow them down. I want to take the prisoners into town after dark."

Marker cocked an eye at the prisoners. "That dangerous, huh?"

"Maybe not them," Rowry replied. "But they've got a lot of friends in Hays. I don't know what their friends might try."

"I'll slow it down," Marker said.

Rowry saw to it that the prisoners were boarded again, then sat down beside Garfield. "Feel any better after your nap?"

"Worse," Garfield grunted. "I always wake up feeling like the stage ran back and forth over me."

"Well, it'll be over by night," Rowry consoled him.

"Not for me," Garfield growled. "You'll be home, but I've got to get back to Dodge. Any of those sandwiches left?"

Rowry handed him the sack, and Garfield dug one out. He bit into it, and a look of distaste touched his face. "They're getting stale."

"I imagine so," Rowry said. "They've had time to dry out. You can throw it out."

Garfield shook his head. "I know I sound crabby. These damned stage rides get to me." He shifted to ease his buttocks. "The ache always starts back there and spreads."

Rowry couldn't help grinning. "Pity poor Lem. He rides these things for a living."

"I wouldn't have his job for anything," Garfield said passionately. "I guess he's armored his rear end so that he can stand it. Say! Why are we slowing down?"

"I told Marker I didn't want to get into Hays until after dark. He's ahead of schedule."

Garfield bit into the sandwich, chewed, then swallowed. "That means more hours of this," he growled.

"Yes, but tonight you'll be sleeping in a real bed," Rowry pointed out.

Garfield refused to be appeased. "Yes, only to wake up in the morning and go through this all over again."

The long afternoon wore on. The sun dipped below the horizon just as the stage went through La Crosse. Rowry knew this country well. They were only a little over twenty miles out of Hays. Marker was one hell of a driver; he picked a time when he would arrive, then hit it right on the nose.

He glanced at the prisoners. Something was beginning to drain them. Their faces were heavier, and they barely exchanged a word. They knew where they were, too. They were near home, but it aroused no jubilation in them. They knew what lay ahead of them.

You stupid bastards, Rowry thought, then dismissed all such thoughts from his mind.

It was dark by the time they reached the outskirts of Hays, and Rowry leaned out the window to shout directions to Marker. "Turn to the right, then straight ahead for about a mile. I want to stop in front of the jail."

"Gotcha," Marker shouted back. He yelled some words at his team that Rowry missed.

The stage pulled up at the jail. A light was on in the office, and Rowry was grateful for that. Creed was still up.

He stepped down, forcing his stiffened legs to obey his command. "Hold them a minute until I see that everything is ready. Butler doesn't know I'm coming."

He looked through the window before he entered the room. Creed's head was down on his arms. He was asleep.

Rowry let the door slam behind him, and the noise jerked Butler awake. He raised a heavy head and stared at Rowry with sleep-fogged eyes. "Rowry," he shouted and struggled to his feet. "I'll be goddamned. It's really you."

"The last time I checked it was," Rowry said. "Come on outside. I've got something to show you."

Butler followed him to the stage, and Rowry ordered, "Look inside, Creed."

Butler did, then said in an incredulous tone, "You found them." At this hour, most of the town was asleep. The street was empty. "Let's get them inside, Creed, before somebody comes along."

Butler nodded and helped herd the prisoners inside. He even shoved Verl through the doorway. He closed and locked the door behind him. "You had them shackled pretty good."

Rowry nodded. "Once I had them I couldn't take any chance of them escaping. Lock them up, Creed."

"Shall I remove the iron?"

Rowry considered that, then said, "Maybe the leg-irons after we get them in a cell. Leave the handcuffs on."

He and Butler came back into the office carrying the leg-irons. "Creed, this is Frank Garfield, one of Masterson's deputies. Bat sent him along to be sure those three would be under a watchful eye all the way. This is Lem Marker, the best driver I ever knew. Take Frank and Lem to a hotel so they can get a night's sleep. They've got to go back in the morning."

"So you found them in Dodge," Butler said admiringly. He wanted to talk more about it, but Rowry said firmly, "We'll talk after you get them bedded down. Lock the door behind you."

Butler looked crossly at him. "You didn't have to tell me that."

He followed Garfield and Marker out the door, shutting it behind him emphatically.

Rowry grinned as he sat down at Butler's desk. Butler could be a crusty old codger at times. He took the money out of his crammed pockets, straightening it out as he did. He had just finished when he heard the door being unlocked.

He got up from Butler's desk and asked, "Get them fixed up?"

"They'll be as cozy as babies." Butler was still cross. "Now, will you tell me a few things? You were gone so damned long I was beginning to stew."

"Sorry about that, Creed," Rowry said gently. "I looked for them in Wichita and Abilene with no results. Then I moved on to Dodge. My money ran out, and I took a job as a swamper."

"A swamper?" Butler asked indignantly. "You didn't have to do that. You could have let me know."

"I was out of money. Bat found me at my new job. He didn't like it, either. He forced me to leave." He grinned at the memory. "Made the owner of the Long Branch Saloon pretty unhappy. You know, I learned something. I could make a living at being a swamper."

Butler choked on an oath. "Go on," he ordered.

"Bat had an idea how we might find those three. We tried it and it worked. We waited outside a whorehouse. On the third night, those three came walking up."

"How did Bat know how to pick the right house?"

"A special girl worked there. Bat said he never had seen such a build on a woman in his life. Talk about her was all over town. Bat thought it might draw three young bucks."

"Did you see her?" Butler asked with renewed interest.

Rowry shook his head. "I never did."

"That's too bad," Butler said.

"It didn't interest me that much," Rowry said simply. "Look at your desk."

Butler turned his head, and his eyes bugged out at the neat little piles of money. "Looks like you stopped by to rob a bank."

"That came from a bank robbery," Rowry said and grinned. "That's what the three had in their pockets after we picked them up. A little over seven thousand dollars. I guess they spent the rest of it. Take good care of it, Creed. I want to give it back to Wellman."

"I wouldn't do a damned thing to help him," Butler snorted.

"Oh, it won't be any help," Rowry assured him. "I want you to do one more thing for me, Creed."

"Name it," Butler said.

"I want you to go around and tell some people you want them here at the office at nine o'clock in the morning. Don't tell them why. That'll be my pleasure."

"Name them."

"You may have to wake up some of them. I don't give a damn. I want Judge Chambers, Kilarny, Mayor Reaves, Wellman and Charley Tucker. I'll do the talking. You know, I'm looking forward to that."

Butler finished jotting down the names and chuckled. "Looks like you intend to rub some noses in the dirt. I don't blame you. I'll be back as soon as I can. Rowry, don't tell me to lock that damned door again."

Rowry looked in at the cell before he settled down. The three must be plumb worn out, for all of them were asleep. Poor kids, he thought again and shook his head. None of it was his doing.

He came back to the office and settled in a chair. He put his feet up and closed his eyes. He didn't really want to fall asleep—not yet. It would be too hard to awaken him.

He kept dozing, then his eyes would fly open. It must have been the better part of an hour before Butler returned.

"Did you get in touch with all of them?" Rowry asked anxiously.

"Every one, Rowry. It took some time to awaken a few of them. But every one of them will be here at nine o'clock. You didn't have Kearns on your list. I debated about including him, then decided against it. I figured you knew what you were doing."

Rowry grinned. "I don't need Kearns. It'll get back to him soon enough. Creed, I'm going to take the cot next to their cell. I want to be close if they even so much as cough."

"You don't have to do that," Butler protested. "I'm going to be here."

Rowry tried to talk him out of staying, to no avail. "All right, Creed," he said. "If that's the way it has to be. Call me when all those people get here."

He went back to the cell, left its door open, and settled himself on the cot. They were still asleep. He could hear the soft rumbling of their snoring.

He didn't know what time it was when he awakened. Maybe it was the opening and closing of the outer door that had gotten through the heavy fog of his sleeping. Damned but he felt good. This was going to be a glorious day.

The buzz of talk from the office carried to him. One voice sounded particularly angry. "I demand to know why you ordered me down here, Marshal. My bank opens at nine o'clock. Neither Charley nor me will be there to open the doors. By God, you're going to pay for this."

Rowry knew who was speaking even before Butler said wearily, "Oh, shut up, Wellman. And stay that way."

Rowry heard the indignant splutterings. It had been a long time since anybody had talked to Wellman like that.

"Rowry," Butler called. "Time to rise and shine."

Rowry heard the startled ejaculations coming from the others. It'd take him a moment longer before he could answer any of their speculations. He unlocked the cell door next to his and said, "Come on, get up. Judgment Day has arrived."

He herded them down the corridor and kicked open the door to the office. He let the handcuffed prisoners enter first.

He followed them into the office and said, "Good morning, gentlemen. I'm glad you could be here to greet our special visitors. I don't have to introduce any of them."

He looked squarely at Wellman, and if he ever saw a man wilt visibly, he was looking at one now. Wellman's face had turned ashen; he looked like a death mask. His hands were shaking, and he couldn't speak.

But Charley Tucker could. "Oh God, Mr. Wellman," he wailed. "They know everything."

"Shut up, Charley," Wellman said furiously.

Judge Chambers took charge. "I'd advise you to do the same, Mr. Wellman. Rowry, tell me what happened."

Rowry recounted the capture in Dodge. "They had over seven thousand dollars in their pockets. Creed has it."

Butler unlocked his desk and pulled out a thick sheaf of bills.

Wellman collapsed into a chair. "That's my money. I'm—"

"Ah," Chambers said knowingly. "Then you admit there was a bank robbery."

Wellman held his head in his hands and rocked it back and forth. "Yes, there was one," he admitted in a hushed voice. "My God, Judge, what else could I do? My son was involved. To protect him, I took money out of my own account and put it with the bank's funds." He was babbling and couldn't stop.

"You know what you've done?" Chambers asked sternly. At Wellman's nod he said, "Mr. Kilarny, I think you can list the charges."

Kilarny's eyes were dancing. "I think I can, sir. For a start, there's conspiracy between Mr. Wellman and Mr. Kearns. Kearns had to know what was going on. Second, there was perjury on the witness stand. Third and worst, he jeopardized the welfare of another human being. Done deliberately, I might add. I can probably add a dozen more, but that's enough for a start."

Chambers nodded gravely. "An excellent start, I'd say. It ought to bring the people involved a long term. Mayor Reaves, you had a part in this. You accused Rowry of being a liar. You fired him."

Reaves looked ghastly. "How did I know, Judge? I only went on what seemed apparent. I'm sorry."

"Hardly much of a repayment," Chambers said sternly. "I'd advise you to re-establish Rowry immediately."

"Not enough," Butler said. "I'm resigning. I'm getting too old to be put through this kind of harassment. Hays is without a marshal."

"Mayor," Chambers said firmly. "I'd suggest you appoint Rowry marshal of Hays. With a sufficient raise in pay."

"I'll do it, sir," Reaves said brokenly. "Consider it done."

Chambers eyed him speculatively. "I don't think the voters will think very highly of your performance when this news gets out. You'd better enjoy your high position until the next election. I don't think it will be there when that election happens." He glanced at Rowry. "Anything else, Rowry?"

"One other thing," Rowry said. "Bat Masterson of Dodge sent me back in a stage, hired solely to transport the prisoners, along with one of his deputies to guard against any possibility of escape. I think Bat should be compensated for his outlay."

"By all means," Chambers agreed. "Mayor, I recommend you pay for whatever Rowry asks for. Oh, another thing. I think you should hire a new prosecutor immediately. Mr. Kearns hasn't proven he's adequate."

"That'll be done, sir," Reaves assured him.

"Anything else to wind up this distasteful business, Mr. Kilarny?" Chambers asked.

"I think Mr. Wellman should be locked up until he can be brought to trial along with his son and the other two. As for Mayor Reaves and Charley Tucker, they're small fish, hardly worth keeping."

Chambers nodded. "I'm inclined to agree with you. Now, if that winds up everything, I'm going to have my breakfast." He stood and looked severely at Mayor Reaves. "Mayor, if Rowry tells you to do anything, I'd suggest you jump. You may be able to make up a little for your stupidity, though I doubt it. Rowry, the town will be happy to have a thoroughly reliable man keeping the peace. Good morning, gentlemen," he said and walked out of the office.

A babble of talk broke out when he was gone. "Mr. Wellman ordered me to say nothing if anybody asked me about a robbery at the bank," Tucker said. "I was afraid to go against his orders."

"We understand," Rowry said. "Forget it. You can leave now if you want."

Tucker scooted out of the office, relief washing over his face.

Rowry turned to Reaves, and his face wasn't friendly. "We don't need you any more, Mayor."

"What else could I do, Rowry?" Reaves begged. "I didn't think a prominent citizen like Wellman would lie to me."

"You didn't think very hard, did you?" Rowry said in disgust. "Get out of here."

The office quieted down after the two left. Wellman tried once more. "What would any of you have done if your son had been involved? I couldn't do anything else."

"For God's sake, shut up," Butler roared. "On your feet, all four of you."

"Where are we going?" Wellman wailed.

"You're going to get a taste of being locked up," Butler said firmly. "You may know a little of what Rowry went through. Move. All of you."

He herded them out of the office, and the faint clang of two cell doors drifted back to Rowry.

"Life worth living again, Rowry?" Kilarny asked, smiling broadly.

"You don't know how much," Rowry said fervently. "Jeff, I want to thank you for everything—"

Kilarny cut off the rest of Rowry's words with a slash of his hand. "I enjoyed every minute of it. I'm only going to miss one thing."

"What's that, Jeff?"

"I won't be around to see the sick look on Kearns's face when Reaves fires him." He shook his head and chuckled. "Well, a person can't get everything he wants out of life." He crossed over to Rowry and gripped his hand. "I'm glad you're back in the saddle, Rowry."

"Two of us, Jeff." He felt a lump in his throat as he watched Kilarny leave the office.

Butler came back and hung up the keys. "Never heard so much wailing and cussing in my life. Between Wellman's begging and cussing out his son, a man could hardly think. His kind always scream the loudest."

"Creed, you didn't have to resign," Rowry said earnestly.

"The hell I didn't. I thought about it all the time you were gone. I want to sit back in peace. Only one official chore I have to do."

"What's that?"

"Mind the store while you tell Abby what's happened. She'll want to know, won't she?"

"She will," Rowry said, his eyes shining. He stopped and looked back from the door. "I'll see you around, Creed."

Butler settled down in a chair. He looked happy. "You bet you will. I'll be coming around to point out the mistakes a greenhorn makes."

Rowry was laughing as he went out of the door.

He couldn't get to Abby's house fast enough, and his heart was thumping furiously as he went up the walk. He hammered on the door, and it seemed an eternity before Abby opened it.

"Rowry," she said, her eyes rounding in shock. "I didn't know where you were."

"You couldn't have," he said gravely. "It's all over, Abby." He related everything that had happened, and her breathing quickened.

"Then all our worry is over?"

"Over," he said solemnly. "On top of all that I got a promotion. I'll be carrying the marshal's badge. Creed resigned. Nothing I said. He just wanted it that way."

"Oh, Rowry," she sobbed and fell into his arms.

He spent the best portion of the remaining day at her place. "I've got to go by my house, Abby," he said. "It's been so long since I've had a bath and a change of clothes, I must smell like a goat."

"Then it's a smell I like," she said, laughing. The old radiance had returned to her eyes.

Rowry kissed her, then said, "Abby, there's no reason why we shouldn't be married now."

"None in the least," she said. "I've only waited for you to say when."

"I only waited until I was sure I could afford a wife," he replied. "I can now. Will you marry me?"

"Oh, Rowry," she sobbed. "I'm considering that as a promise."

"As good as gold," he said and laughed. "I'll be seeing you soon."

"I'll also hold you to that promise."

"I expect you to, Abby."

He walked to his house, wondering at how everything had turned out so well from such a bleak start. He considered himself the luckiest man in the world.

He frowned as the knob turned under his hand. He was sure he had locked this door when he left. Oh well, it didn't matter. There wasn't much crime in Hays. Rarely did somebody attempt to enter another's house without permission.

He walked into the parlor, and his jaw sagged. "Pa," he said hoarsely.

Sid looked around, and he looked so frail. Rowry could swear he had lost fifteen pounds. "Couldn't get along with Edith," Sid grumbled. "I thought I'd come back and see if you'd take me back. That was only a couple of days ago. I decided to wait for you." Tears slowly began leaking out of his eyes. "Rowry, can you ever forgive a stupid old fool? I was all wrong about Ord."

Rowry swallowed hard. "So you've heard about me bringing in the other three. They had part of the money on them."

"So there was a robbery, and Ord was in on it with them. It's all over town what really happened, Rowry," Sid said, squinching up his eyes to cut down on the flow of tears. He was sobbing now, and it was becoming more difficult for him to speak. "I don't see how you can ever forgive me, Rowry. I've been such a blind old fool."

His distress was making Rowry uncomfortable. "All of us make mistakes, Pa." He forced a steady grin. "If we didn't, we wouldn't be human."

"No," Sid said, shaking his head violently. "I saw a lot of things that I'd overlooked. Plain stubbornness, I guess. I wouldn't listen to you. I wouldn't have listened to anybody. I saw that Ord was going bad, and I refused to admit it, even to myself. Just a stubborn, blind old fool, Rowry."

Rowry walked over to him and put a reassuring arm across those bony shoulders. "It's all over, Pa," he said, and his laughter sounded a little shaky. If they didn't end this maudlin scene soon, he would be laughing through tears.

"You mean you're forgiving me?" Sid asked incredulously.

Rowry chuckled. "I'm stubborn that way. Heard some more good news this morning. From now on, I'll be the marshal of Hays with an increase in pay. To top that, I asked Abby to marry me, and she said yes."

Sid's tears had stopped flowing. His eyes were beginning to shine. "You've got a stubborn streak," he accused Rowry. "And you got it from me."

"Don't I know it?" Rowry exclaimed. "It's not a bad trait at certain times. How about me fixing you the best meal I can make? I've been gone several weeks. I don't know what we've got in the house."

Sid smiled shyly at him. "You know I'd consider myself a lucky man to have anything you fix."

Rowry was humming to himself as he set about finding something fit to eat. The last distressing bit in his life had been removed. He was the luckiest man in the world.

About the Author

Giles A. Lutz was the author of many Western stories and novels, among them *The Feud, The Great Railroad War, Killer's Trail,* and *The Echo.* His novel *The Honyocker* was the winner of the Spur Award for Best Western Novel. Mr. Lutz died in 1982.